Life of a Savage

Romell Tukes

Lock Down Publications and Ca$h
Presents

Life of a Savage

A Novel by *Romell Tukes*

Romell Tukes

Lock Down Publications
P.O. Box 870494
Mesquite, Tx 75187

Lock Down Publications
Like our page on Facebook: Lock Down Publications @
www.facebook.com/lockdownpublications.ldp
Cover design and layout by: **Dynasty Cover Me**
Book interior design by: **Shawn Walker**
Edited by: **Mia Rucker**

Stay Connected with Us!

Text **LOCKDOWN** to 22828 to stay up-to-date with new releases, sneak peaks, contests and more...

Thank you!

Submission Guideline.

Submit the first three chapters of your completed manuscript to ldpsubmissions@gmail.com, subject line: Your book's title. The manuscript must be in a .doc file and sent as an attachment. Document should be in Times New Roman, double spaced and in size 12 font. Also, provide your synopsis and full contact information. If sending multiple submissions, they must each be in a separate email.

Have a story but no way to send it electronically? You can still submit to LDP/Ca$h Presents. Send in the first three chapters, written or typed, of your completed manuscript to:

LDP: Submissions Dept
P.O. Box 870494
Mesquite, Tx 75187

DO NOT send original manuscript. Must be a duplicate.

Provide your synopsis and a cover letter containing your full contact information.

Thanks for considering LDP and Ca$h Presents.

Acknowledgments

First, I would like to give thanks to the most high Allah, of course… I would like to give a shout to my pops and uncles riding this bid out with me, since day one, behind these federal walls. One time to all the good men that pushed me to keep writing, like Kensari City – Murder, New York – OG Chuck family, Boston – Heff, Harlem – Young Sauce, Queens – Big Stokes, BX – Henny, BX – Humpy, Philly Westside – Neef, Philly Chester – Jabril, Yonkers – Smurf, Fresh, CB, Lingo, YB, SG, Smoke Black free dat real… I will keep busting my pen. They can never lock my mental down. Last but not least, shout to LDP for giving me a shot when nobody else would. This is only the beginning. Stay tuned…

Romell Tukes

Prologue

February 10, 1990

Big Tone was in the King County Hospital in Brooklyn, New York, awaiting the birth of his son. Lisa was his soon-to-be baby's mother, as well as the love of his life.

Lisa was sweating profusely as she shouted at the top of her lungs. The doctors thought the devil was coming out of her.

"What the fuck are you smiling at, you burnt motherfucker? Come get this damn baby out of me," she yelled.

The African doctor did his best not to laugh at how Lisa was reacting to her pain. In his head, he'd been called worse.

At that very moment, life couldn't have been moving any slower for Lisa, who was in such pain.

"You have to push, Lisa," the doctor spoke in a heavy accent.

"What the fuck you think I'm doing? Aww!" Lisa couldn't bare the pain.

Tone was in the hallway, leaving Sam, his best friend, a message, telling him to come to the hospital. Tone had also just hung up with Jessica, Lisa's best friend, whom Tone had been fucking.

Tone had been ducking Jessica lately. He had finally realized how crazy she truly was. She'd been blowing up his phone, leaving threatening messages about telling Lisa about their affair.

Tone knew Lisa wouldn't hesitate to kill both of them, if she ever found out.

As soon as Tone walked back into the room, the smell of blood hit him, causing him to gag.

Lisa gave him a stare that could've taken his life if her eyes were a gun. "I'm going to fucking kill you," she growled.

"Push, Lisa, push," the doctor coached. "Give me one big push on three."

After twenty minutes of sweat, blood, and tears, and some cursing, Lil' Savage was born.

"Tone, look at our son," Lisa said in a low whisper. Exhaustion took over her entire body.

Tone was the happiest man alive, and at that moment, he knew making Lisa his wife was for the best, being that she was the total package as a woman.

"Thank you so much, Lisa." Tone had tears in his eyes as he looked down on his son.

Lil' Savage hadn't even cried as he entered this cold world.

"Baby, I'm going to run out to my truck. I have a surprise for you," Tone said.

"Hurry back."

"I love you, Lisa," stated Tone.

Tone walked out, leaving those words echoing in Lisa's ears. Those words would be his last.

Chapter 1

Before the Savage

Big Tone grew up in Brooklyn, East New York, in the Pink Houses projects.

Growing up, Tone was known for his violent ways, and his anger. Having to grow up in those projects was hard for any child. Tone had a hard-working mother, who was raising him and his two brothers. His father was never around, due to his addiction to gambling. He was what Tone called a distant father.

Tone's two brothers became strung out on drugs, leaving Tone to wonder if he would be another statistic for society.

At the age of seventeen, Tone started making a serious name for himself by robbing drug dealers.

By the age of eighteen, he caught his first state bid, which was twenty years for robbery and two attempted murders.

He served most of his time in prisons, such as Sing Sing, Clinton, Auburn, and Attica. Big Tone became a Muslim, not out of fear, or for protection, but because it was his calling.

Tone spent his time studying and working out in the prison yard. He came home at the age of thirty-three, and that was when he met Lisa.

Lisa was twenty-six years old at the time. She had graduated from college and gotten her degree in the medical field. The two met in a lounge in Manhattan on a hot summer night. Tone was by himself.

Lisa was with her best friend, Jessica, as they eyed Big Tone.

"Girl, I wonder who that sexy, dark skin dude is over there looking like an almond bar," Lisa said.

They both laughed, but they had no clue. Unbeknownst to them, Big Tone's heart was darker than his skin.

The young ladies smiled and stared at Big Tone. He felt the stares as he turned around, seeing two beautiful women. He was especially intrigued by the woman with the hazel eyes.

Being the player he was, he knew how to read females. He knew they were feeling him, so Tone made his way over to them.

Lisa stood, unable to feel her legs. She was stuck, like a deer in headlights.

"Damn, girl, I think he's coming over here. How do my breath smell?" Lisa said, blowing her breath toward Jessica's face.

Jessica made a sour face before saying, "Damn, girl, I think I got some mouth wash or toothpaste in my purse."

Both women laughed as Big Tone approached. Their hearts skipped a beat, due to his massive size, as they looked up at the 6'5" frame with 280 pounds of muscle.

"Good evening, ladies. I'm Tone, and normally I don't do this, but I couldn't help but to admire your beauty. I would like to know your name."

"My name is Jessica."

Big Tone looked at her, causing her body to become covered in goose bumps. "Nice to meet you, Jessica, but I was talking to my future with the hazel eyes."

"I'm Lisa, and this is my best friend, as you now know."

"Do you mind if we take a walk and talk?" Tone asked.

"Sure, why not?" Lisa answered. "Jessica, I'll be right back," Lisa told her friend as she made her way to the bar area with Big Tone.

After about fifteen minutes of talking and laughing, Lisa felt comfortable around Big Tone. She found him to be hilarious. He made her feel like a true woman in such a short time. Big Tone said things that saturated her panties.

Jessica was still standing in the corner waiting for a man to approach her so she could laugh, just like her friend was doing with Big Tone.

Big Tone took a liking to Lisa. He felt as if she was a good girl with a nasty side.

Tone checked his watch, seeing that it was late, so he went for the kill. "Lisa, do you have any plans for the night?"

"No, not really. Why do you ask?" Lisa bit down on her bottom lip, looking into Big Tone's eyes.

"I would love to invite you to my apartment so we can finish enjoying ourselves." Big Tone smiled, showcasing all thirty-two perfect white teeth.

Lisa thought about saying no, but she was truly having a really good time with him, so much so that she didn't want to let him go.

"Hold on, let me go tell my friend I'm leaving." Lisa walked over to Jessica. "I'm going to chill with Tone. I'll get with you tomorrow."

"Bitch! You just met him," Jessica retorted.

"Don't be mad. I'm about to have a real man. Remember, it was you who wanted me to get out the house. Better yet, bitch, you need some dick!"

Jessica burst out laughing, knowing those were her words. "You better be careful of that dick, 'cause that nigga is packing a nine or better."

"Bitch, how you know?" Lisa asked with a raised eyebrow.

"I was dick print searching."

"Un-un. You better keep your eyes off of my man's dick. That dick belongs to me," Lisa said, high-fiving her girl.

"Make sure you call me in the morning. I want the 411," Jessica said.

"Definitely," Lisa replied, hugging her friend before walking away.

***

Tone and Lisa arrived at his apartment about thirty minutes later. Lisa made herself at home in his apartment. This was something she never did.

Lisa was tipsy and horny, and Tone was it. But they still talked a lot about Malcom X, MLK, Rosa Parks, and what was going on in society.

Big Tone was impressed by how intelligent Lisa was. Lisa was also impressed by how smart Big Tone was. Lisa definitely loved a smart man.

The two stared in each other's eyes as Lisa rubbed Big Tone's muscular arm. She leaned in and ignited the kiss between the two.

Moments later, she was undressed, baring her creamy unblemished skin with her legs spread wide.

Big Tone stared at her clean shaved pussy that revealed her camel toe. Lisa didn't know how he stroked himself to full erection.

Big Tone entered a tight Lisa, who screamed at the top of her lungs, even though Tone didn't fully enter her. As she got used to his length and width, the two made love for over two hours. Big Tone made Lisa cum six times, until the sun came up.

Chapter 2

Lisa

Lisa grew up in a rich family. Her father was a Dominican drug lord and her mother was an honorable housewife.

Lisa grew up on the Eastside of Manhattan as the only child. She'd had a silver spoon in her mouth her entire. Lisa only had one friend. Jessica wasn't just her friend, but her sister. They did everything together growing up.

A lot of kids didn't like Lisa because she was pretty and had everything she ever wanted. Lisa and Jessica had been friends since elementary school.

Jessica was the total opposite of Lisa. She grew up with four other siblings, all younger than her, and a mother who was a prostitute with a heroin addiction. She was miserable, broke, and a gold digger.

Unlike Jessica, Lisa graduated from Princeton University, while Jessica barely made it through high school. Now, both at the age of twenty-six, Lisa was ready to settle down and build a family. As for Jessica, she wouldn't be ready to settle down until she could trap a rich man into her web.

Lisa was a RN at the major hospital in the city, and Jessica was a CNA, which in the hood's eyes was a regular hood rat career.

As Lisa awoke with a hangover, Big Tone was in the kitchen cooking. Lisa smelled all types of aromas. The smells had actually woken her up.

"Good morning, sexy," Big Tone said, looking her up and down before walking into his bedroom.

Lisa smiled before saying, "My pussy is sore. I think you ripped a wall."

The two laughed as Tone brought her breakfast in bed.

Lisa looked at the bacon on the plate as she sat up. "Is that turkey?" she quizzed, staring at it.

"What?" Tone replied, wanting to smack the hell out of her, but held his composure.

"You must be one of them non-pork eating, wanna-be Muslim motherfuckers," Lisa said laughing.

"I am fucking Muslim. You got a problem with that?"

Lisa stopped laughing at the drop of a dime. "I'm sorry. I had no idea you was a Muslim," Lisa apologized. Changing subject, she asked, "So, who apartment is this? It looks too damn clean, as if a woman lives here."

Big Tone knew women, and he knew she was trying to fish, so he played along to hook the bait. "My wife and kids live here," Tone said.

Lisa's heart damn near scrambled. She wanted to cry. All she could think about was being naked in another woman's bed.

Big Tone smiled. "I'm joking. I got you." They both started laughing. "This is our apartment."

Lisa noticed how he'd used the word *our* freely, causing her to smile within.

"I can get you a maid if you like."

Lisa smiled with her puppy dog eyes looking at Big Tone. "Ours?"

"Yes, ours," he confirmed. "I like you, Lisa. Shit, the pussy is amazing." His words caused Lisa to blush. "I'm at an age where I am ready to settle down."

Hearing that was like music to Lisa's young ears.

"How do you afford a place like this? Because you're doing damn good for a person who just came home," stated Lisa. She then grabbed her plate of food and started eating.

"To be honest, I'm a male stripper."

Lisa was about curse his ass out until he smiled again.

"Boy," she said, taking a bite of her bacon.

"Naw, I'm a security guard for rappers and clubs."

"Well, I still live with my mother," Lisa said.

"Not no more," Big Tone cut her off. "This is your new home now," he added.

All Lisa could do was smile, as if she'd just hit the lottery.

***

Six months passed as Big Tone and Lisa became very attached to one another. It was as if they were soul mates.

Sex was great, their dates were great, and they both had attitudes that allowed their stubbornness to take over. The two knew each other like a book, but there was no denying that the two were deeply in love with one another.

Lisa was out on a lunch date with Jessica in SoHo.

"Damn, you finally coming up for air? What's going on with you and Tone?" Jessica questioned with a raised eyebrow.

"Jess, I am so in love with this nigga. I never felt like this. Tone isn't like these other dudes out here. I have everything a girl could ever want, and I'm not talking about the material shit," Lisa stated before Jessica could fix her mouth to say some dumb shit, like she always did.

"He gives me comfort, and let me not forget that big dick." Her statement made them both laugh.

"Damn, sounds like you ready for marriage?" Jessica retorted.

"Maybe, girl, just maybe. How's things with you?" Lisa asked with a sincere expression.

"I'm lonely and horny. The last nigga I fucked had a dick only his mother could love, and the rest are broke like me or broker," Jessica said with a dead serious look.

"My baby supposed to be security for that big party in the village on Saturday. I wish I could go. I heard it's going to be off the hook," Lisa informed her best friend.

Jessica's thoughts started to run wildly. Unbeknownst to Lisa, her best friend had a thing for Tone. Jessica truly envied her best friend. She was the one who wanted Big Tone, but as always, Lisa was the one men always wanted to holler at.

"What club is it going to be at?" Jessica asked.

"I believe the China Wall. Too bad I have to work. What are you going to be doing?"

"Sleeping, girl. I have to work in the morning," Jessica lied. If only Lisa knew, she would be trying to push up on her man.

Chapter 3

Betrayal

On Saturday night, Big Tone pulled up to the club in his black Tahoe truck. He was ready to work, hoping he didn't have to whip a drunk patron's ass that night.

The last time he was there, a riot broke out and he ended up knocking out two gangbangers and slamming three people on their heads.

Big Tone walked through the doors an hour before the party started to go speak with the owner.

Jamie was the club owner. He was a young, rich white boy, who'd inherited all his family's money when they passed away.

"Aye, big man, long time no speak."

"Don't you mean long time no see?" Big Tone approached with a smile, extending his hand.

"Tomato, tomatoes, same shit," Jamie shrugged his shoulder with a chuckle as he shook Big Tone's hand.

"I just hope tonight won't be a repeat of last time," Big Tone said. Both men laughed.

"Yeah, I hope it goes well tonight," Jamie replied.

The two conversed until it was show time. The club was packed to capacity. There was barely room for a person to walk, let alone dance.

Big Tone found the perfect location to stand and watch the partygoers enjoy themselves. His attention was drawn to the woman who strutted like she owned the club as every man's eyes followed her. If they had the money, she was ready to fuck.

Big Tone stood in awe. His dick was harder than Japanese arithmetic.

Damn, I want that, Big Tone thought to himself before an image of Lisa's face flashed in his mind.

Everyone stared at the beautiful woman who walked straight to the back of the club to watch the atmosphere.

Jessica ignored every man who made cat calls or smiled in her direction. Little did all the men know, she was in that club for one specific person, Big Tone.

Jessica spotted Big Tone by the wall across the club, eyeing her. She made her move. She approached Big Tone, who looked like the cat who'd just ate the canary.

"Do you remember me?" Jessica started over the loud music.

Big Tone stared at her with a confused expression before saying, "No. Should I?"

Jessica rolled her eyes. As if on cue, she turned and started to walk away, but Big Tone grabbed her wrist.

"Got him," Jessica said.

"I'm sorry, but I just came home, and I work security in so many clubs that I forget people's faces. I hardly see women as beautiful as you around, and I definitely would've remembered your face." Big Tone smiled.

Jessica felt her juices running down between her thighs, being that she wore nothing underneath her dress.

"So, refresh my memory," Big Tone told her.

"My name is Ashley," Jessica lied. She didn't want to use her real name since he hadn't a clue of who she was. "Do you mind if we reminisce later. After a hard week of work, I just want to dance and have a drink," stated Jessica.

Big Tone looked around the club, seeing that it was calm, so he took her up on her offer.

Jessica grinded on his third leg all night. Big Tone was so mesmerized and horny that he couldn't talk. He looked at his watch.

Damn, 3:45 a.m. he thought. Fifteen minutes later, the club was closing, and the partygoers were making their way out.

Jessica's night, on the other hand, had just started as she looked at Big Tone in a seductive way. "What's next Mr. Tone?" Jessica questioned, licking her lips.

"Ashley, I have a woman, and I don't want to lead you on."

Jessica loved how the name Ashley rolled off his tongue.

"I guess I'll see you around," she said, spinning off and walking away.

"Ashley," Big Tone called out to her. "Do you need a ride home?"

She smiled before turning around. She knew things were going as she planned them. "Yes, if it doesn't put a strain on you."

"Give me a minute," he said as he went to the back to collect his pay.

After collecting all he had to collect, Jessica grabbed his arm as they exited.

Big Tone was a gentleman. As he opened the passenger door for Jessica, she hopped in with a lot of ass hanging off the seat.

Shit! Maybe a one-night stand won't be so bad, Big Tone thought to himself.

Little did he know, Jessica could be extremely possessive over what wasn't hers.

***

Meanwhile, Lisa was working overnight at the hospital to pull extra hours. She didn't need the extra money, but she damn sure would bank it.

"Why does it always smell like shit at night around this bitch," Lisa mumbled to herself.

Lisa looked up to catch one of the LPNs walking down the hall.

"Hello, Tiff, where you been?" Lisa asked. It wasn't like she cared if she was dead or alive to be honest.

"On vacation, girl," Tiff said. "Plus, I just got married."

Lisa was surprised to hear somebody married the gorilla looking bitch.

"I went to Jamaica for my honeymoon," Tiff smiled.

Lisa stood with a fake smile plastered on her face. She wondered who was crazy enough to even wanna be seen with Tiff.

"I, myself, believe I found Mr. Right," Lisa informed with a smile.

Lisa felt her phone vibrate. When she checked to see who it was, she blushed as if Big Tone stood in front of her.

"Excuse me, Tiff," Lisa said, walking away as she answered her phone. It was against the rules to use a cell phone inside the hospital. "Hello."

"Just wanted to tell you I love you and can't wait to see you," Big Tone said sweetly.

"I love you, too, and keep my smile in its cage."

If only she knew, some snakes are poisonous.

"Woman, bye."

"Bye, baby." The two ended their call.

***

After hanging up with Lisa, Big Tone drove for almost five minutes in silence. Something was tugging at him as he stole glances of the beautiful woman sitting in his passenger seat.

Damn, she does look familiar as hell, but where did I see her at before? Big Tone thought, but couldn't remember.

"Where do you live, Ashley?" Big Tone finally broke the silence.

Big Tone looked everywhere except at her. Jessica noticed a change in him.

"Wherever you wanna go is cool."

"Look, Ashley, I already told you I have a woman, who I love. I can't fuck that up. You're sexy as hell, but I'm loyal," Big Tone stressed.

Jessica's face turned sour, but she wasn't going to give up. "I can't tell by the look of your pants." She pointed.

"I-I-I," he stumbled over his words in embarrassment. "I don't want to hurt you, Ashley."

Jessica leaned over and grabbed his crotch as she whispered into his ear. "I like it when it hurt, daddy," she purred, causing Big Tone to almost crash into a pole.

"Fuck," he yelled out, regaining control of the wheel.

Big Tone's mind was now made up as he did a U-turn and drove to the nearest hotel.

Once they made it to the hotel, Big Tone paid for room 205. They entered the room and their clothes immediately hit the floor. They climbed onto the bed, but not before Jessica grabbed Tone's manhood and took him into the warmth of her mouth. Jessica would speed up and slow down as she played with his balls.

"D-d-damn," Big Tone mumbled.

Jessica's head game was so good, all Big Tone could do was moan every time she sent his dick deeper down her throat, like a pro.

Big Tone's knees grew weak as Jessica placed both hands on his ass and started slamming her mouth against his dick.

Big Tone could no longer hold off. As he let loose his seeds, Jessica swallowed every drop.

Big Tone made sure he gave her three hours of rough sex, causing her to climax six times.

Chapter 4

Caught

Big Tone woke up a couple hours later. He hoped his dream wasn't true. Once he looked to his left, he knew it wasn't a dream. Jessica was sound asleep, looking as if she'd had a rough night. Big Tone checked his phone, seeing that he had ten missed calls, all from Lisa. He was pissed as he jumped up to go take a shower and get rid of the pussy juices that were on him.

Damn, I fucked up. I should've never let her get in my truck, but damn that was some great pussy, Tone conversed with himself.

He hated to admit it, but it was the truth. Big Tone wanted some more of this Ashley chick, but knew she would be trouble.

Then it dawned on him that he went raw and was nutting all up in her like she was Lisa. He definitely knew he'd fucked up.

He walked out of the bathroom with a towel wrapped around his chiseled abs and muscular body, which could have graced the cover of Men's Health magazine.

Ashley was up, staring at him, very impressed with what she saw, and what she and Lisa now shared.

I see why my girl's ass is in love with this sexy ass man, she thought. Jessica's hand fell down to her pussy, which was swollen from the dicking that was put on her.

"Good morning," she said.

Big Tone walked past her and just nodded, pissing her off. She felt like moaning.

"Oh, so it's like that now?" she questioned as she got up to go to the bathroom. Sucking her teeth, she slammed the bathroom door.

Big Tone didn't care for the emotional shit with a female that wasn't his woman. He went to check his messages, seeing two more missed calls. He quickly dialed Lisa, coming up with a lie.

"Good morning, baby. I'm at a breakfast meeting with my boss," Big Tone lied. He hoped it would be believable, knowing he didn't want to lose Lisa over a one night stand.

"Okay," Lisa said, hanging up and causing Big Tone to look at his phone.

Jessica walked out of the bathroom and began gathering her clothes.

"I'm sorry. I'm not a morning person, Ashley."

"I understand, Tone. I like you, and I hope what we had wasn't a one night stand."

His facial expression changed in seconds, not knowing what to say to Jessica, who he knew as Ashley.

"Ashley, I have to go home," he said, changing the subject. "I have to prepare for a long day. Can I drop you off anywhere? I don't want to leave, but I have to work again tonight. This morning was great. I hope to see you soon." Big Tone smiled.

A huge smile came across Jessica's face as well. She was happy to know.

"So, did I please you, daddy?"

"Yes, you did."

"Tone, please give me a chance. I know you're in love with your girl. I'll be number two. I promise I'll be obedient to you, daddy."

Big Tone gave it some thought, knowing it wouldn't hurt now that she knew she was the side bitch.

"Okay. Let's see how it turns out, Ashley. Take my number."

Jessica took his number and kissed him as they prepared to leave.

***

As Tone pulled up to Union Square to drop Jessica off, Tone felt there was something very familiar about her. Then he realized it was his paranoia playing with his mind.

Once he dropped her off, Tone was off to the big house. As Big Tone was driving, he turned the volume up to one of his favorite songs, "My Lady" by Freddie Jackson.

As he pulled into his garage in his complex, he started to wonder if Lisa actually believed his lie. *Why did she just hang up on me?* He thought.

Big Tone made it upstairs, hoping she was asleep. As he stepped into his apartment, he saw it was clean and quiet, as it always was. Walking down the hall to his bedroom, he came to a sudden halt.

"What the fuck," he mumbled.

Big Tone knew his ears had to be playing tricks on him as loud moans came from behind his bedroom door. His anger exploded like a volcano, as he put his ear to the door to make sure he was hearing right.

"Yyyyesss. Oooh shit. I-I'm cuuuming," Lisa shouted.

I know this bitch don't have no nigga in my fucking bed. That's why her ass hung up how she did. Big Tone's heart was crushed. His phone vibrated. As he looked down at the unfamiliar number, he sent it to voicemail.

"Yyyeees." Lisa's last moan was enough to send Big Tone over the edge. He kicked his door in, rushing into his bedroom, only to stop dead in his tracks. He saw a big black penis between his girl-friend's sexy legs. Luckily for Lisa, it was a dildo.

Big Tone's guilt started to kick in. Lisa locked eyes with Big Tone as her moans grew louder and white cream spewed out of her.

After a few seconds of catching her breath, she smiled at Big Tone. "Hi, baby. I need some real dick."

"Baby, I'm a little stressed. Can we do a raincheck? I am having a bad morning."

Lisa looked at him dumfounded. "So, you going to let me waste a good nut, and I've been waiting for you since I got off."

Little did Lisa know, Big Tone's dick was sore. Superhead couldn't get his dick hard on her best day. Jessica made sure she did a number on his dick.

Big Tone tried to avoid her by walking to the bathroom, but she jumped off the bed and was on Tone's ass.

"So, what has you so stressed that you're smelling like a differ-ent soap."

With that, she had his full attention. Unbeknownst to Big Tone, Lisa only bought one kind of soap, so she could detect if he'd been showering at another female's crib.

Tone was in a state of confusion as he slowly turned to face her with an angry expression.

"So, what you trying to say, Lisa? You have my heart and I'm loyal to you, baby. I would never play you. I was at work. Then I had an early meeting, so I put a dab of cologne on," he stated, looking Lisa in her eyes.

Big Tone really thought he'd convinced Lisa, but she wasn't the average female. She saw straight through his bullshit.

"Let me see your dick."

Tone looked as if he just lost his best friend.

"Baby, why you don't trust me? I love you."

"So, show me, Tone."

Once he pulled out his penis, Lisa smelled it like she was a dick detective. She gripped his dick, causing Tone to wince in pain.

She looked up into his eyes. "So, you wear cologne on your dick, too?"

"Yeah, I did it for you," Tone replied.

"What the fuck do you take me for?" She pulled on his already sore dick. "You was fucking. That's why you don't want to fuck me. And you have the nerve to have your boxers on backwards." Lisa grew furious as she gripped his dick even tighter, sending Tone to his tippy toes. "Don't call me or leave me any messages until I am ready to talk to you." She released his dick and went to get dressed, leaving Big Tone speechless. He was caught and he was to blame.

Chapter 5

Jessica

Jessica woke up around noon in her twin size bed, the same bed she'd been sleeping in for twenty-six years. She was raised in her mom and dad's home, so she was a homebody with a crazy body. Jessica's father was murdered when she was ten, by her uncle. Boo Bear, Jessica's father, was a con artist and a bank robber.

Her father and uncle did a bank robbery in D.C. and came out with over $150,000. Her father only gave his brother, J-Bo, $20,000. Once they made it back to Miami, J-Bo killed his brother and took all the money. He was caught three years later in New Jersey, where the FBI sentenced him to six life sentences.

Since the murder of her father, things had been hard for her mother, who turned to drugs and prostitution to take care of Jessica and her siblings.

Jessica hated her life and hated her mother, who would use Jessica's beauty to bring money into the home, and just to keep a roof over their heads.

Maria felt Jessica's body was worth more than her paycheck, so she and her daughter would turn tricks together.

Jessica realized what time it was and started to prepare to get up for work. She walked to her small bathroom to shower and get herself together, as she always did.

Jessica looked down at the white man, who was snoring, feeling ashamed and lost. All she could think about was why did her life have to be a complete disaster.

After showering and kicking out her trick, she looked in the mirror to admire her thick curves.

"Damn, I'm sexy," she said as her mother barged into her bedroom.

"Where's my money?"

"Your money?" Jessica looked at her mother like she was crazy.

"Yeah, bitch, my percentage. I know Steve spent his normal amount, which $150. Give me my $75."

This bitch done lost her mind, like I'm her hoe, Jessica thought. "You didn't lay on your back to collect any money."

"Bitch, I'm keeping a roof over your damn head, and I fucking take your ass to work. Shit isn't free," Maria stated.

Jessica didn't want to argue with her mom, being that it would lead to them throwing blows. She peeled off $75 and tossed it at her mother.

"You better have that rent money on Friday or your black ass will be getting warm over a garbage can in an alley," her mom snarled. "And bring your ass on before you lose this job. I'm not your taxi either." Maria walked out.

I can't wait to get my own shit, Jessica thought as she wiped away her tears. Her mind drifted to Big Tone and how she'd had multiple orgasms, causing her to be hooked like a drug.

Chapter 6

Sam

Big Tone hopped out of his truck with his workout gear and his gym bag, ready to get busy with his workout partner.

"What's good, big man?" Sam asked.

"Slow motion," Big Tone replied.

Sam had been a good friend of Tone's since they were behind the wall upstate in Five Points Correctional Facility, where they were cellmates.

Sam stood 6'1" with brown skin, weighing 225 pounds. The ladies loved Sam, but he had jungle fever.

Sam been out of the joint for a little over a year, and his career as a personal trainer was going well.

"How about we do chest and legs today?" Sam said.

Big Tone shrugged his shoulders, not really caring at all. He just wanted to get to the workout.

"I'll follow your lead," Tone stated.

"Are you sure, because you're looking stressed out for some reason?" said Sam.

"No, I'm good. Let's get this money," Big Tone reassured him, though he was anything but good. His mind was on Lisa. She hadn't called him or left a message. Even though she told him not to contact her, he went against her wish. It had been a week since she'd been gone, and Big Tone had left almost 200 messages begging her to come home. His begging and pleading went unanswered.

Sam warmed up with 225 pounds on the bench. Both men worked up to 405 pounds for 10 reps.

"Sam, I'm pretty sure I can trust your judgement, being that you never led me wrong."

Sam stopped working the dumbbells to listen to his friend. "I'm all ears," Sam said.

"I have a good woman, very loyal, but I fucked up and cheated with a bad bitch I met in the club, and I got caught. I left about 200 messages and she's not returning them."

Sam knew it was serious between Big Tone and this woman because he never stressed anything.

"She smelled my dick, and to make matters worse, my boxers were on backwards."

Sam balled over in laughter, causing everybody in Golds Gym to look over at them.

Big Tone stood there as his friend clowned him with tears in his eyes.

"Are you done, Sam, because I need help?"

Sam grew serious, seeing his friend's desperation.

"Okay, but you know you fucked up. Why would you cheat then go home to your girl. With your boxers on backwards, at that?" He chuckled, wiping away his running tears. "What I would do is kiss her ass, wait on her hand and foot, and fuck her like your life depended on it. As far as the substitute, don't deactivate her just yet. Keep her at arm's reach because she might be a crazy bitch," Sam explained.

Big Tone listened as he tried to memorize everything Sam was telling him. Then his phone vibrated. He snatched it from off his hip, hoping it was Lisa, but it was Ashley.

"Hello."

"Hey, I left a pair of earrings in your truck. Can you bring them to my job on 138th and St. Nick?"

"I'll be by." He ended his call, pissed off. How could he still be careless?

Big Tone told Sam about the call as Sam shook his head. Sam knew this new chick was going to be a serious problem.

An hour later, both men were done with their workout. Working out was a routine that was Monday through Friday at their regular time, just like it was for them in prison, bright and early.

Sam had a different life outside of the gym. He was a connect to all the hustlers. He was moving bricks of dope all through the Tri-State, but only his clients knew he was the man.

Chapter 7

Surprise

Big Tone left a message to Lisa. He confessed his love and how he messed up and would never do it again.

Big Tone was driving to Harlem to meet with Jessica to drop off her earrings.

Jessica was at work waiting to go on her lunch break, but first, she had to wipe her patient's ass. Ms. Evans was an elderly lady, who weighed over 315 pounds and never listened to any of her nurses.

"Ms. Evans, can you please turn over so I can wipe you?" Ms. Evans looked at Jessica as if she was a ghost. "Please, just turn your big ass over. I know you hear me," stated Jessica

Once she realized Ms. Evans wasn't going to give in, she took matters into her own hands. Jessica grabbed her from behind to try to roll her over on her bed. As Jessica pushed, she realized how heavy the fat bitch really was.

Ten minutes after wiping and sweating, Jessica was done and ready to take her lunch break. She walked to the park across the street from her patient's house and called Big Tone, giving her location.

Five minutes later, he pulled up and parked. Once he got out and walked over to her, Jessica saw his muscles poking out everywhere. She instantly became wet.

"You left these?"

"Yes, thank you. They cost a lot."

Big Tone laughed to himself because he knew them shits was faker than a stripper's ass.

"No problem. How's work?" Tone asked.

"It's cool. I need a new job and a new life. Tone, I'm going to be straight with you, I'm lost without you and I want to know where we go from here. I told you I'll play my role, if you let me."

"Okay. I'm going to Cali for 2 weeks. When I come back, we can work on us, 'cause I'm feeling you also," stated Tone.

A smile grew across her face. She was happy to hear that because she thought it was a one night stand. The two kissed and went their separate ways.

***

Lisa finally returned Big Tone's call once he returned from Cali, making him the happiest man in the world. She felt as though she had punished him enough for his mistake and agreed to give him another chance.

After working on their relationship for several months, Big Tone and Lisa were preparing to celebrate their ten month anniversary, or so he thought. Lisa definitely had more for him than he expected.

Lisa had a surprise for Big Tone, which she'd been holding back from him. Big Tone was in his prayer room, making Maghrib prayers, as he faced the East, towards Mecca.

One thing for sure and two things for certain, Big Tone didn't miss prayer. As he walked out of his room, he saw Lisa in the kitchen eating peaches.

"Hey, baby, how was prayer?"

"It was good, as always, Lisa."

Lisa loved the fact that Big Tone was deep into his religion and that he stood for something.

"I have a surprise for you, daddy."

Big Tone's eyes grew wide, because he wondered if the surprise was about Ashley.

The chemistry had been great between Tone and Ashley, but she'd been acting very jealous and crazy lately. Tone was starting to have feelings for Ashley a little bit, but he wouldn't allow his feelings to go any further because he was in love with Lisa.

"Baby, you know I don't like surprises," Big Tone started.

"I'm pregnant," Lisa revealed with a huge smile.

Big Tone felt like he was just hit with a ton of bricks. He stood speechless.

"Tone, are you okay?"

"Yes," was the only thing he could say. "How long have you been pregnant Lisa?"

"About 5 ½ weeks. Why? Are you mad?"

"No, baby, I'm going to be the best father I can be."

"I know you will. I want you to know that you're about to have a family and I don't want no bitch ruining it."

"You don't have to worry about that ever happening again," he said.

What Big Tone wanted to really say was "who's the father," but he went against it.

"I can't wait to tell my friend, Jessica. We going to throw a huge baby shower."

Big Tone plastered a genuine smile across he face, seeing how innocent Lisa was.

What would I have been thinking to ask her is it my baby, knowing how loyal she's been? I love this fucking woman to death.

"Daddy, I love you, and I never want to lose you. I will forever have your back, no matter how hard it gets. We overcome shit together." Those words penetrated Big Tone's heart as Lisa kissed him and led him to the bedroom to go make love.

Chapter 8

Parole Officer

Big Tone had just got done making his morning prayer before the sun came up. He then realized Ramadan was approaching soon.

Big Tone had been stressed out lately, mainly because of his unborn child and Ashley's craziness. Tone's parents had passed away years ago, and his brothers were doing worse than he was, serving life in prison.

As Big Tone got ready to start his day, he remembered he had to send his brother, Travis, some money.

Big Tone always tried his best to take care of friends and family. He was a really good brother. Tone woke Lisa up for work.

"Good morning, baby. You have to get ready for work," he said while shaking her.

Lisa got up and walked to the shower in her birthday suit, with her breath smelling like dog shit. Tone couldn't help but laugh.

Lisa had been having second thoughts about keeping the baby. Lisa also knew if she got an abortion, her father would roll over in his grave.

"Baby, can you come here please," she shouted out to Big Tone.

Big Tone walked into the smoky bathroom, shaking his head.

"Yeah, boo, what's up?" he leaned against the sink.

"Are you sure you want to keep the baby? I don't want to force no child on you. I can have an abortion," stated Lisa.

Big Tone stepped over to the shower, staring her dead in her eyes. "I'm a man. You're my woman. You didn't make this baby alone. Do you understand me?"

"Yes, I understand."

"Never, and I mean never, question my love or loyalty for our family. Now hurry up so you don't be late."

***

As Big Tone drove Lisa to work, he pulled over at a corner to mail his brother's money order.

"I been so hungry lately, I can eat a cow," Lisa announced.

The two laughed, pulling into the McDonald's drive-thru to order breakfast.

"Baby, I cannot wait to get off tonight."

"Why?" Big Tone looked over at her.

"I want some dick tonight. Baby, I be so wet at work, I have to bring an extra pair of panties," Lisa said.

"Then it's a date, boo. I'll pick you up later. I gotta go see my PO, then I'm going to hit the gym."

"Okay. I'm going to have lunch with Jessica, my best friend. I want to tell her the good news."

Once they got their food and he dropped Lisa off at work, Tone rushed to the parole building, so he wouldn't be late.

When he arrived, he saw an all-white Benz with a beautiful white chick inside. All he could do was laugh because he knew it was Sam.

Big Tone walked in to get searched, and proceeded to the clerk's desk to check in.

"I'm here to see Ms. Johnson."

The woman looked up at him coldly. "Okay, and you want a cookie? Sign in and sit down," the clerk said, annoyed. Big Tone wondered how could a lady so ugly be so mean. Her overbite and showing bumps looked nasty.

Big Tone walked over to Sam to have a seat. Sam was just finishing up a phone cell.

"What's up, big man? I hope you ready for this pain in the gym today," said Sam, smiling.

"I'm always ready, Sam, believe that," Tone replied. Minutes later, a couple of parole officers came out calling parolees' names. Just so happened, both men were called at the same time. Once in Ms. Johnson's office, Tone had to admit she was beautiful with no flaws.

"Have you been arrested? Police contact? Drug use? Or have you had a change of address since you been released" she asked.

"No," Tone said sharply.

"Good, because you have life parole, so if you even jaywalk, I will send your black, muscle-head ass back to prison where you will wash socks and draws for a living," Ms. Johnson said seriously, looking him up and down.

Big Tone left her office, taking a deep breath, knowing she needed some dick.

Romell Tukes

Chapter 9

Crazy Emotions

It was time for Lisa's lunch break. She couldn't wait, knowing she had been thinking about food all day. Not to mention, her emotions were like a rollercoaster at Six Flags.

As Lisa made her way towards the exit of the hospital, Jessica was sitting in her mom's car in front of the hospital. Lisa got in the car to see Jessica staring at her oddly.

This bitch put on some weight, Jessica thought, but she kept her thoughts to herself as she pulled off.

Moments later, when they pulled up to the restaurant, Lisa felt her stomach kick.

"I see your crazy mom let you use her car," Lisa said.

"Yeah, for a fee, as always," Jessica said, as both women laughed and made their way inside the restaurant.

Once they sat down, they ordered their food, which was steak, rice, and shrimp for both of the ladies. After their food came, they began to talk and eat, just like old times.

"I have a surprise for you," Lisa said.

Jessica continued to eat her steak, wondering what kind of corny ass surprise her friend had for her.

"I'm pregnant," Lisa said proudly.

Jessica began to choke on a piece of meat. She grabbed a glass of water before she died.

"Wow, that's, ummm," Jessica paused for a minute, trying to think of what to say. "I'm happy for you, if that's what you want," Jessica said.

Lisa shook her head with a smile. This made Jessica cry, but her tears were tears of pain and anger, not happiness.

"Why are you crying, girl?" Lisa asked, wondering what was wrong with her best friend.

"I'm just so happy for you," Jessica said with a fake smile, while wiping away her tears.

Lisa knew her friend and she could feel something was very wrong with Jessica, but she just brushed it off.

***

Tone called Jessica, telling her to meet him at 7pm in Union Square, in the city of New York. Tone hadn't seen Jessica in more than three weeks, and for some weird reason, it was killing him.

Lisa was getting annoying and under his skin lately, and she was turning him off. Jessica was in her room getting ready to see Tone, so she was looking for something sexy to wear. Jessica felt less of a woman for what she was about to do, her best friend's soon to be baby's father. Jessica stood in her mirror, wishing she was the one. Then an idea hit her.

Jessica ran to the bathroom and threw away all of the birth control pills in the cabinet, with an evil grin.

Tone was about to exit his building, looking sharp in his Armani suit and Kangol hat. Tone saw his PO coming towards him in full speed, but he played it smooth. He still had an hour left before his curfew. Ms. Johnson looked Tone up and down, surprised, she licked her soft lips.

"Damn, you must be busy tonight," Ms. Johnson said with a smirk.

"Not at all. Why you ask?" Tone said with a grin. "You look beautiful, as well. I'm sure your husband is at home waiting for you right now," Tone said.

"Nigga, please. I'm single and living life. Don't let this job fool you," Ms. Johnson said. "I'm not going to hold you up. Make sure you report in two weeks and I am going to be watching you closely," Ms. Johnson said as she walked off.

Once his PO left, Tone walked to his truck, thinking he may soon have a chance to fuck his PO.

***

About twenty minutes later, Tone pulled up in front of Union Square to see Jessica standing there looking sexy in her Dior sky blue dress, with high heels, waiting on him.

Jessica climbed in his truck and greeted him with a kiss on the cheek, but with an attitude. Tone felt the vibes but kept quiet as he drove to his favorite food spot.

The ride was silent. You could feel the tension in the air. You could've cut it with a knife.

"Did I do something to you, bitch, for you to be sitting in my shit with an attitude," Tone asked Jessica, whose name he thought was Ashley. She was shocked to hear him call her out of her name.

"What? Nigga, you got me fucked up. Your mama a bitch, you green mile looking bitch," she shouted while pointing in his face. "You lost your fucking mind. I'm not one of your fucking bitches," she said, getting extra hyped.

"I'm sorry. I'm just stressed, but I really miss you," he said as he pulled into his favorite soul food restaurant.

"Yeah, I bet," she replied as she exited his truck, making her way into the restaurant. Tone grabbed his pistol. He never left home without it because he didn't trust a soul.

Once inside, Jessica was amazed at how big and clean the place was. The waiters were serving all types of food on trays. Jazz music could be heard in the back, and the candle lights gave the place a better atmosphere.

Tone opened doors for her, and pulled out her chair, making her feel special, but she could only image how many times he'd taken Lisa there.

After their food arrived, they talked for about thirty minutes before Tone thought it was the perfect time to drop the bomb.

"Ashley I want to be honest with you because I do love you, but my girl is pregnant, and I don't know what to," was all he could get out before Jessica tossed a glass of wine in his face.

"Damn, it's like that. I'm sorry. I fucked up. I wish I can have you both," he said, wiping his wet face with a napkin as the wine stained his outfit.

"Nigga, you smoking base? You got the wrong bitch," Jessica stated, trying to hold back her tears.

Conversation was limited for the rest of the night, but that didn't stop them from going to a hotel to have a night cap.

Tone admired her wide hips and curves in her dress as she walked towards the hotel room, swaying her hips, trying to seduce him.

"I don't have no panties on, and I'm soaking wet," she said as soon as they made it into the room. She wasn't too mad at Tone after a couple of cups of wine, plus she know what is was.

"I am going to freshen up," she stated, taking off her heels while he sat on the bed, like a little kid on punishment.

Forty minutes later, she stepped out of the shower with nothing on, except a pair of lace thongs stuck between her pretty waxed pussy lips.

Jessica wasted no time in sucking his massive dick. She loved every taste of it. After she swallowed all of his bitter taste, she rode his dick until the sun rose.

The two made love for hours, until they fell asleep in each other's arms, as if they were a real couple. She woke up to a letter from Tone, letting her know how much he loved her and that he was in a hard place.

Chapter 10

Off Guard

A couple of weeks passed and things were going smoother than ever. Lisa and Tone found out they were having a baby boy.

"I think we should name him Randall. That was my grandfather's name. He was a good man. I don't want my son to have my name. I want him to be able to have a new everything when he comes into this world. I want him to be nothing like me," Tone stated, while they were both relaxing in their bedroom.

"I agree, baby," Lisa replied proudly. "I need money to go shopping for the baby shower, and I'm getting so fat," Lisa said, rubbing her stomach while eating cookies and cream ice cream by the gallon.

"Ok, here," he said, pulling out a stack of hundred-dollar bills and handing it to her before he went in the next room to make his night prayer.

***

Harlem

The next day Lisa used Tone's truck to go shopping. She had to pick up her friend, Jessica, to spend time with her, because her pregnancy had her distant from everyone.

Since Lisa's car was in the shop, she was using Tone's truck for the time being. She felt as if everything in her life was coming together. The only thing she was missing was a ring, but that was her next goal.

Lisa pulled up to Jessica's building and called to inform her she was outside waiting. Minutes later, Jessica walked downstairs, wearing tight jeans and a blouse. Niggas stopped to get her attention, as they did every day.

Jessica hated the Lincoln Projects. Growing up in the hood was like growing up in a jungle, and the niggas were lions on the hunt.

She saw Tone's trucked parked in front of a fire extinguisher, but she knew it was Lisa because she'd called.

Jessica got in the truck to see Lisa had a funny look on her face, as if she smelled something sour.

"Hey, girl, what's up? I ain't seen you in so long. Why the long face?" Jessica asked while Lisa pulled off into traffic.

"I'm good, but how did you know it was me? My car in the shop, girl," Lisa stated, catching her off guard.

Trying to think of a fast reply, Jessica stated, "Oh, girl, don't nobody park in front of a fire extinguisher," she said, feeling a little uncomfortable, as if her friend knew something.

The ride was regular, with small talk as the lyrics of Whitney Houston played in the background.

"I can't wait until I build my own family," Jessica said proudly as they pulled into the large mall parking lot.

"I'm ready for this baby, and to settle down with Tone. I love him till death," Lisa stated as Jessica's face became angry and full of envy.

***

The mall was packed with shoppers as they shopped for the up-coming baby shower. Lisa couldn't stop talking about having a boy because she knew boys were more attached to their mother.

Lisa spent over $1,500 in an hour. She'd already made two trips to the parking lot.

"Lisa. Lisa," was all the two women heard as they walked through the Gallery. Lisa turned around to see who was calling her. To her surprise, it was her ex-boyfriend, Jason.

"Hi, Jason, it's nice to see you," Lisa said flatly as she looked at his missing teeth and dirty clothes. The two broke up when she found out he was stealing money from her to buy crack.

"I'm okay, but it's been rough. Hope to see better day," he said as they smelled his breath.

"I see," Jessica said, holding her breath while Lisa shoved her arm telling her to shut up.

"You got one on the way, I see," he said, looking at her tummy poking out.

"Yeah, a boy," she said, feeling sad for him.

"Can you spare some change?" he asked with his head down, showing the bald spot in the middle of his young head.

"Sure, but please, Jason, stop using. Get help," she said as she handed him a fifty-dollar bill before she walked off, disappointed.

Chapter 11

Baby Shower

Sam and Tone left the gym early because Tone had let Lisa use his car to get to around until her car was ready, which should've been sometime that week.

"You coming to the baby shower?" Tone said, breaking the silence in the Benz.

"Of course, big man. I wouldn't miss it. And I see you got a lot on your mind," Sam said as he focused on the highway.

"Yeah, but everything is everything," Tone replied.

The two talked until they made it to the lower Eastside area, where he dropped Tone off. Then he hopped on the highway. Sam had an important meeting to attend to in an hour.

***

Tone went to work later on that night, and Ashley (Jessica) paged him all night. She needed some dick, and he planned to give it to her as soon as he got off.

With so much going on, she was his only stress reliever, and he needed it. Plus, the pussy and the head game was off the hook.

***

Saturday approached quickly, and Lisa had the baby shower prepared and rehearsed to the T.

The guest arrived before one at a nice classy ballroom in Westchester. The food was catered by Blacks Soul restaurant, and they did a great job. Food covered three large tables.

People were showering her with gifts. Lisa had lots of friends showing up. The place was packed. People she didn't even know were bringing her gifts.

Lisa wore a DKNY gown, and Jessica wore a mini skirt, looking like a hoochie going out to a club. Jessica prayed Tone would show up so she could finally see the damn look on his face. It was judgement day.

"This shit is off the hook, girl," Jessica shouted over the LL Cool J song blasted by the DJ.

"Yeah, thank you for your help. I couldn't do it without you, girl," Lisa replied, thinking about Tone because he was supposed to be there thirty minutes ago.

***

Tone and Sam both entered the ballroom, looking like money in their cream suits.

"This is nice. Look at all the beautiful women," Sam said, looking around at all the beautiful women. "I'm leaving with something today," Sam said, laughing.

"Nigga, this a baby shower, not a club," Tone said as he saw Lisa sitting in a chair made for a queen. He made his way over to her.

Lisa saw Tone approaching her and she tried to hold her smile back, but she was not familiar with the brown skin brother he was with.

"Hey, baby, sorry I'm late. Traffic is crazy on the GWB," Tone said, kissing her soft lips.

"It's ok, you hear now and the food is delicious," Lisa said, eating a piece of cake.

"You did great. This is my friend Sam I was telling about," he said, introducing the two.

"My friend, Jessica, is in the restroom. I've been waiting for you to meet her forever. I don't know what's taking her so long," she said as Jessica appeared from the back with a diva walk.

Tone thought his eyes were playing tricks on him, but when he saw it was Ashley, his blood boiled.

"Hey, I'm Jessica, nice to finally meet you," she said with a fake smile, as Tone tried to hold his composure.

"Baby, you okay?" Lisa asked, feeling something was wrong. "You look spooked," she added. "You don't remember Jessica from the first night we met? Anyway, Jess, that's his friend, Sam," said Lisa as she saw Tone start sweating like never before.

"I am going to smoke. I'll be back," Tone said.

Tone and Sam walked away, leaving Lisa with a confused expression on her face.

"I can't believe this bitch played me like that," Tone yelled.

"Who? What are you talking about?" Sam asked as he watched Tone pace the parking lot.

"Man, that Jessica bitch is Ashley, the bitch I been fucking, that pretty bitch with the phat ass, son," Tone stated.

"Well, I guess I can forget about asking you to put a word for me," Sam said with a laugh, as Tone gave him the evil eye.

"This shit not a game. She best friends with my baby mother. I fucked myself," he yelled. "I gotta end this shit now," Tone said as he called her phone, only to get her voicemail, so he left a message.

Tone as Sam left without going back inside. He was ready to kill that bitch, but he had to play his cards smart before his secret was exposed to the real love of his life.

Chapter 12

Diamonds are Forever

Tone started to work double shifts, just to bring in extra money for the baby. Lately, Jessica was blowing up his phone like a terrorist, but he refused to answer it. Overall, everything was going as planned for the couple.

***

Brooklyn, NY

Sam sat at his brother's gravesite, drinking Henny out the bottle, on his BK shit.

"I promise I am going to get who did this shit to you," he said with tears as he slowly stood up, almost falling back down.

Sam stumbled to his car. He was on his way to one of his side bitches' cribs to relieve some stress.

***

Jessica had been locked in her room for days, crying and thinking about suicide.

"How can this bastard do me like this? I hope he dies," she stated, sitting on her bed next to a bottle of prescription pills she'd been using to ease her pain.

Since the baby shower, her life was going downhill. Drugs were her only escape.

***

Diamond District

Tone approached the large jewelry stand with one thing in mind, a perfect ring for Lisa. It was time he popped the big question.

There was a pretty, young, white female working. She was wearing a three-piece suit and had long blond hair.

"Can I help you, sir?" the young saleswoman said with a bright smile.

"Yes, a good friend of mine named Jamie told me to come down here to purchase a wedding ring, but he told me to ask for Becky Logan to assist me," he stated. He watched her smile turn into a frown as her face turned beet red.

"You go tell that piece of shit, Jamie, to fuck himself and burn in hell," she said strongly. The other customers looked at her as if she was crazy.

Tone figure out quick who Becky was, but he still needed a ring.

"I'm sorry. I just hate that nasty fucking bitch, but what type of ring you want? I'm sure I can help," she said taking a deep breath. Tone explained to her that it was an engagement ring, and she took him to the perfect ring. The ring was big, icy, and at a good price so he wasted no time paying for it.

Chapter 13

Labor

Lisa's stomach was hurting for some odd reason. She couldn't figure it out, but that didn't stop her from looking for a new home on the computer.

Her dream was to move to Miami and have a good life, where it's sunny, with no snow. Lisa hadn't heard from Jess since the baby shower. Her phone was off and Lisa wondered if she was ok.

Within seconds of sitting down, Lisa had to pee, but before she could even make it to the restroom, her water broke. She was able to grab the phone and call Tone. Luckily, he was down the block, on his way home.

Once he arrived, he left the truck running as he ran to her aid. When he made it inside, she was on the floor. He picked her up with ease and made his way to his truck.

They made it to the hospital in the nick of time. The doctors rushed her into King County Hospital in a wheelchair as she screamed in pain. Once in the room, the doctors and nurses wasted no time as they told her to push.

"Ms. Braxton, push, please," the ugly African doctor yelled. Tone stood in the corner, watching the whole scene unfold, until he felt his phone vibrated. When he saw the number, he stepped out of the room.

"What the fuck you want?" Tone answered.

"I'm pregnant, baby, and I'm sorry," Jessica yelled, hoping for forgiveness.

Tone gave her the dial tone after he heard the word pregnant. He couldn't believe what he heard. He had a feeling she was lying to get his attention. Staring at his phone, he saw Sam had left a voicemail. Tone had called him minutes earlier. When he checked the message, Sam was telling him that he was on his way.

"You want to play phone games? Help me push your damn baby out," Lisa yelled with red eyes as she continued to push, sweating like a female slave in the field.

***

Three hours later, the beautiful baby was delivered. Eight pounds and healthy, Randall Braxton was born on February 10th in King County Hospital. Tone held the small baby in the palm of his hand while he called the Aden in the baby's right ear. "I will only worship Allah and follow His message, Muhammad," he spoke in the Islamic Arabic language.

When he passed the baby back to Lisa, he knew she was the woman he wanted to spend the rest of his life with.

"Baby, I have a gift for you. I am going to run outside to get it," Tone said as he kissed her crusted lips.

Lisa felt as if she was on top of the world. Now everything was perfect.

Tone stepped outside, feeling a little breeze as he walked to his truck, thinking about what Jessica said. When he made it to his truck, he felt a cold piece of steel press against the back of his bald head.

"Turn around and keep your fucking hands up," the gunman said. Tone did as he was told, slowly turning around. There was something about the voice that was familiar, but he couldn't put his hand on it.

"You can't be serious. Sam, what the fuck is up?" Tone said, pissed off.

"Save all that bullshit. I've been waiting for this day. You remember Black Knowledge from East New York that you robbed and killed?" Sam asked, his breath reeking with a strong scent of liquor.

Tone had to think hard, he had robbed and killed so many niggas that he had a lost count. After minutes of thinking, it hit him. Black Knowledge was a big time D-Boy from the Pink Houses that he'd shot in the hood, behind the projects.

"Yeah, I remember that bitch nigga, and I killed your uncle, Judy, that same week," Tone said.

Sam got even angrier because he never knew what happened to Judy. Everybody thought he went back to the Islands.

Sam couldn't take it anymore. He shot Tone in the head six times. Then he ran off as the security guards ran outside after the loud gun fire.

Civilians also heard the noise from the downstairs lobby, but they really paid it no mind. They were waiting on help. This was everyday life in the hospital, packed with all types of different emergencies and issues.

In the lobby, dressed in a new work uniform because Lisa had gotten blood over his other outfit, stood the African doctor who'd delivered Tone's son a short while ago. The doctor was at a loss for words for the John Doe, who'd arrived dead. Not that this was an irregular occurrence, but the African doctor wondered how could Tone be dead in less than twenty minutes, after just seeing him smiling and joyful for the birth of his son.

He thought it would only be right for him to personally deliver the news to the crazy bitch upstairs.

Lisa was under the hospital sheets when she saw they ugly doctor enter again with a disappointed look upon his face.

"Is the baby ok? Is something wrong?" Lisa asked nervously.

"No... but I'm sorry to inform you that the child's father was just murdered in the parking lot," he said.

"Noooo, please, nooo," Lisa cried out and started to wild out, making nurses run into the room, trying to calm her down.

Lisa felt as if her life had just left her body. Losing Tone was unbearable. Now who would help raise her son? Another young, black, beautiful woman forced to be a single parent.

Romell Tukes

Chapter 14

Young Savage

11 Years Later
North Miami

"Randall, hurry your ass up before you be late for your first day of school, and I'm not playing," Lisa yelled from downstairs as his alarm sounded.

"Okay, mom, damn," Savage yelled, hating when his mom called him his real name. He got himself together as he threw on his Nike tracksuit and Air Max 95 shoes to match. He was fly for his first day back to school.

Savage fixed his room up, because if he didn't, Lisa would spazz out on him and whip his ass. She didn't play a dirty house. After he was done, he looked into the mirror and smiled before he threw on his backpack. He was only eleven years old and standing 5'9" in height, with a nice build and long dreads. He was very handsome. All the little girls around his way loved him. He was ladies' man.

Lisa moved to Miami for a new start. After Tone's death, she felt like the walls were closing in on her. She'd found out her best friend, Jessica, was pregnant by Tone. She'd also had the baby. To make it worse, Tone's murderer was still on the loose. She took every penny she and Tone had saved up and moved to Miami, where she became an RN in one of Miami's biggest hospitals.

She was thirty-nine and beautiful. Lisa was thick, and curvy, with flawless skin, a flat stomach, toned body, and a youthful face. Savage walked into the kitchen to see Lisa sitting on a stool, shaking her head at his tight sweatpants. He'd told her it was the new style.

"What time you get off, man?" Savage asked, making a bowl of Rice Krispies cereal.

"Why, Randall?" she replied, gathering her work shit, just in case she had to do another double.

"I just want to know," he stated.

"Just be home on time and don't go nowhere until you do your homework. Education is all a black man has in this crazy world." She paused, and then added, "One of your friends called, and Jada's mom did, too. She forgot today was the first day," Lisa said with a laugh. "I believe Britt called, your little girlfriend."

"Mom, come on, that's a lie. We cool," he said.

"Boy, please, you always smiling when that little girl come around," Lisa said, being honest.

"I am going to be late for school," he said, changing the subject quickly as he climbed off the stool, ready to leave.

***

St. John Middle School

Savage hopped out of his mom's BMW coupe, looking like a star, with his dreads hanging.

"I love you, baby," Lisa yelled out the window. Mom, come on. I'm too old for that," he said, while walking into the cafeteria to meet with his best friends, as they did every year.

Derrick, aka Big D, was a good kid with a rough life. His father was dead and his mother was a coke head, living in poverty. He was overweight, but he was good at football, and he was smart in school, unlike the rest of the crew.

Jordan Smith, aka Bama, was originally from Alabama, but he'd grown up in Miami with his father, Big Curt, who was a hard worker. His mother was sick from cancer and had died years ago. Bama was the wild one of the crew. He and Savage were the closet of the crew. Then there was Britt, she was the Tomboy of the crew.

"Damn, where you been at? I've been calling you all week," Bama asked Savage, walking down the school hallways.

"I've been sleeping, to be real. Look at Big D coming our way," Savage stated as Big D approached them, eating a honey bun and wearing the same clothes he'd worn the previous school year, which he'd outgrown.

"I hope I get the same teacher," Big D said, reaching the bulletin board to see who had which teacher and homeroom class.

"Big D, come by my house after school. My mom got something for you the other day, in your size," Savage said. Big D nodded his head.

All of them had the same class. Ms. Lopez, which was great. Now they could horseplay all day. As soon as they walked into the colorful classroom, with small desks with nametags, they saw Britt waving to them. They were all sitting in the same row.

"Glad you can make it. Please have a seat in your assigned seat," Ms. Lopez said as she turned around from the board. Ms. Lopez was beautiful. She was Spanish, young, and slim, with a round ass, long hair, and a nice face.

Britt was happy to see Savage. She'd seen his name on the bulletin, so she knew they were in the same class.

Brittany Jones was born and raised in Miami. She was a tomboy, but beautiful. She was high yellow and pretty, with green eyes, long hair, and very smart. Britt's parents were both killed in a deadly car crash when she was younger, so her brothers raised her. One brother, Mice, was sentenced to eight life sentences in the feds. Her other bother, Meech, was killed in a drive by a couple years ago. Mice killed the driver and two gunmen, which landed him in prison.

JoJo was the only brother who was alive and free. He was a kingpin, and he'd basically been raising his sister since he was a kid.

"Why y'all dummies so late?" Britt asked Big D.

"If Ms. Lopez teach the way she look, I may learn something," Bama said.

Britt looked at Savage's outfit and smiled. He was fly, as always.

"I would like to know everybody's name and what you want to be when you grow up. Let's starts with Mr. Derrick Williams."

"I'm Derrick, and I want to be a football player," Big D said.

"Ok, good. How about you, Jordan Smith?"

"I want to be a gangsta like Scarface," Bama said, making everybody laugh, except Ms. Lopez.

"Do I need to call home?" she asked. "How about you, Randall Braxton?" she asked, pointing at Savage.

"I want to be successful," Savage said.

"Well, how do you plan to achieve that?" she asked.

"By any means. I'm young, but I want power, money, and respect," he stated sharply.

"Good luck on that," she said, somewhat confused.

"How about you, Ms. Jones?" she asked Britt, who rolled her eyes.

"A female basketball player," she said.

"Ok, this is good. I see we have a lot of athletes and gangstas in here," she said, making the kids laugh as she continued to go around the room.

Chapter 15

Man Down
Five years later

Savage's name was like Freddy on Elm St. in Miami. He was a young gangsta, but not too many people knew his face. He was sixteen with bodies under his belt, and Bama wasn't far behind him. Big D was now 6'3" and 230 pounds, all muscle. He was a high school linebacker and one of the best tight ends in the state.

Things had changed over the years. They'd grown up quickly, even Britt. She was not yet fully developed, and already making teenagers go crazy. But she was a virgin, and she planned to hold on to it.

Savage woke up late. Luckily his mom was at work because she would have tried to force him to go to school, but it wasn't in him anymore.

He had plans to fuck with Bama, so he fixed his bed and got dressed. Then he called a cab to go across town, near Bama's crib.

Savage took a cab to a store a couple of blocks away from Bama's crib. He knew he was home because Bama had dropped out of school and already gotten his GED. He walked around the 7-Eleven and noticed a Middle Eastern man watching his every move.

"Let me get a box of swisher sweets and five Laffy Taffys," Savage asked. As the Muslim clerk handed him everything he asked for, Savage gave him a five dollar bill and walked out. He let the clerk keep the change, letting him know that all black people don't steal.

Savage saw a blue Impala sitting on 30-inch rims. *Whoever that is, he's ringing clean*, Savage thought to himself.

Boo hopped out looking like money, with two big MPM chains and designer clothes from head to toe. Boo was a low-level weed dealer, but his brother, Pole, was a boss. He was the leader of the deadliest crew in Miami, the MPM crew.

Savage watched Boo's every step as he came up with a plan. As Yung Jeezy blared throughout the gas, station Boo came out of the store to pump his gas. He was bopping his head up and down.

"Yo, Boo, what's up, bruh? I need an onion, bro. I heard you had some fire shit, shawty," Savage said as he approached.

Boo recognized the boy's face from around the area, so he told him to get in.

"You Bama, right?" Boo asked, remembering the boy's name.

"Yeah," Savage said, lying and going with the flow

"Everything is in the trunk. I am going to pull in the alley because everything is in my bags. Hold on," Boo said, pulling into the alley behind some abandoned homes.

Boo hopped out, popped his trunk, and fumbled through some duffle bags before he closed it and climbed back into the driver's seat.

He tossed the ounce of purple Kush in Savage's lap, but when he looked at him, he almost pissed himself. A pistol was aimed at his head.

Boo thought he was in a movie. He'd never been robbed because niggas was scared of Pole, but now he was face to face with a gun.

"Please, man, I'm not really a street nigga," Boo admitted, hoping it would save his life.

Savage smiled like a kid at Chuck E. Cheese.

"Give me everything, you bitch ass nigga," Savage said calmly.

"Do you know who my brother is? He will kill you and your family, little nigga," Boo said, trying to sound tough.

Savage laughed while checking Boo's pockets for money, drugs, and guns.

"Don't worry about Pole now, because you got five seconds to give me everything," Savage said seriously.

Boo's mind was speeding. His first thought was to run, but to where.

"I'm not giving you shit. Suck my dick and balls you…" Those were Boo's last words before Savage shot Boo four times in his head. Boo's brains were all over the windows, steering wheel, and floor.

Savage took the keys and got out. He popped the trunk, where he found three duffle bags filled with money, drugs and guns. Savage's eyes lit up like a Christmas tree. He wondered, *how dumb can a nigga be to travel with all this shit.* Savage got back in the car to wipe it down with a rag he'd found. He also took Boo's wallet and walked off slowly toward Bama's crib, carrying three duffle bags, as if nothing happened.

Chapter 16

Startup Kit

Bama was deep in some young pussy in his bedroom. "Yes, daddy, fuck me. Yes. Ahhh. Ahhh," Jada moaned and squirmed as Bama fucked her from the back.

"Take this dick, bitch," Bama said as he pounded her, while grabbing her shoulders like handlebars. Once Bama nutted all inside of her, Jada felt her young legs tremble as she caught her breath.

Boom. Boom. Boom. Bama heard a loud noise coming from the front door.

"Who the fuck is that?" Bama yelled. "Jada, can you go get that?" Bama said as he put on his boxers and hid his gun under the pillow.

Jada put her booty shorts on and exited the room to answer the door. She hoped it wasn't the police because she was only 15 and knew she would be in trouble. Jada was young with a body of a grown woman. She only fucked with Bama to get closer to Savage. She was in love with him. Jada had ass hanging out her little shorts as she opened the door. Savage walked right past Jada, as if she wasn't even there. Jada closed the door and followed behind Savage, smelling her breath and fixing her hair.

"Hi, Savage. Where you been? I been kinda worried about you," said Jada as Savage walked into the kitchen to get a soda.

"I'm good, shawty. You should put some clothes on," Savage said, looking her up and down. "Why you worried about me? Ain't you fucking Bama?" Savage said coldly.

"I only do it to get closer to you," Jada said as she put her head down sadly.

"Well that's a hell of a way to get to me. Who next, Big D?" Savage said as he walked towards Bama's room, leaving Jada in tears.

She felt her chance with Savage was done because of her mistake. She didn't even like Bama. He was too rough and overly aggressive.

Savage walked in Bama's room to see him lying in his bed watching Godfather II, smoking a blunt. "I know you not in here cuffing Jada's young ass, bra," Savage said as he dropped the duffle bags on the floor.

"Naw, we just chilling. Plus, that bitch is always asking and talking about you, like she the police," Bama said with a smile. "That bitch fuck and got a bod like a stripper," Bama added, laughing.

"What's that in the bags?" Bama asked as he raised up from his bed to be nosey.

Jada entered the room to see what was going on. She saw blood stains on Savage's jeans, but she didn't say anything as she went to sit down. Savage and Bama stopped talking as they both looked at Jada oddly.

"Did I do something?" Jada said, feeling the uneasy tension in the room.

"Do you think you can go home, Jada, because me and Bama got to handle something?" Savage asked her.

Jada saw the heavy bags on the floor as she picked up her clothes and shoes. As she left the room, Savage pulled out a hundred-dollar bill from one of the duffle bags, and then followed Jada towards the door.

"Jada, hold on," Savage yelled.

"Yes, Savage," Jada said, hoping he would walk her home.

"Here, take this and be safe," Savage said as he handed her the money with a friendly hug.

Savage closed the door behind Jada and locked every lock that was attached to the door.

Bama was dressing in his Dickie jeans and Black Label shirt, with his long dreads tied to the back. Savage walked back into Bama's room and went straight for the duffle bags with a bright smile on his face. Savage emptied every duffle bag on Bama's bed. When he was done, the bed was covered with drugs, money, and guns. Bama was so shell shocked that he couldn't even move. He was at a loss for words.

"I'ma make sure we never struggle or sell for no nigga," Savage said proudly. "We bosses, bra. You can't be a boss and a worker," Savage continued.

"Damn, where you get all this from? How you go on a lick without me?" Bama said, admiring the pistols and the assault rifles.

"You know Boo soft ass?" Savage asked, smelling the pounds of weed that laid on the bed.

"Yeah, Pole's brother," Bama said, looking confused.

"Well," was all Savage said.

"What they got to do with this?" Bama asked nervously because he knew their reputation in the streets.

"This was all Boo's shit," Savage said as if it wasn't nothing.

"You know they gone come at us hard, bra. But no matter what, I'm down for you," Bama said.

Bama knew it was about to be a war. He'd seen Savage kill a man over twenty dollars, so he knew his friend was a loose cannon. He even witnessed Savage kill a couple because they didn't empty out all their pockets. He just hoped he knew what they were up against now.

"Don't worry about Pole. I'm doing my research on him now. Plus, I got Boo's ID, so somebody lives here," Savage said, pointing at the ID with the address 48 Maple Road on it.

"Frist, we need to get a strong team of youngins. I hope Big D and Britt are down because we about to be on some next level shit," Savage said.

Bama just nodded his head in agreement. He knew what came with this lifestyle and he was ready. Bama knew Savage better than anybody, and he was always meant every word he said, even if he was joking. Both men sat in their own thoughts, staring at the things that people lived and died for in life: money, drugs, and guns.

Chapter 17

Da Team

Jada was walking down the street with two things on her mind, Savage and the money he'd just given her. She thought it would be wise to spend it on clothes instead of taking it home because her mom would either steal it or talk her out of it.

Jada's mother was a crack-head who would do anything to get her next hit, literally *anything*. She even sold her daughter over twenty times for sex so she could get drugs. Nobody understood why Jada was fast, or always looking for love from males to replace her hurt or emptiness. She was brown skin, had long hair, and was thick for her age. She was absolutely beautiful at the age of 15.

Jada was walking down the street lost in her own thoughts until she saw red and blue lights everywhere with caution tape around a crime scene.

***

Britt and Big D couldn't believe what they were watching. They were on their way from school, heading to Bama's house. All of the police cars, ambulances, and yellow tape had the whole neighborhood out being nosey.

"Damn, Big D, look like they putting the white sheet over that boy," Britt said, poking him.

"Yeah, I know. I can see. And that Impala looks kinda familiar," Big D said as he tried to put two and two together.

"Oh shit, Britt, that's Boo's shit, Pole's little brother," Big D said.

Britt tried to look at his face. It did look like him, if she subtracted the bullet holes. Once the sheet covered his face, people started to walk off. They all continued on with their usual business as if nothing had happened. Bodies dropped in Miami like flies drop in the summer. That was just how it went.

As they were ready to leave, Britt saw a familiar face approaching them, which made her smile turn upside down. Jada rolled up on them with a spaced-out look on her face.

"Hi, guys, y'all saw Boo died, too?" Jada asked.

"Yeah, that shit crazy, Jada. He was cool," Big D said.

Britt just rolled her eyes as if she hadn't even noticed Jada standing there. She knew Jada had a thing for Savage, and that didn't sit right with Britt.

"I feel sorry for Boo. They shot him like eight times in the head, from the looks of it," Jada said.

"I feel sorrier for whoever did this. MPM going to turn the city up again, just like when Lil Ray died," Jada said.

"Yeah, it's going down," Big D said.

Big D saw the attitude on Britt's face. She looked like she was ready to curse a bitch out, so he said his good-byes and they walked to Bama's crib.

"Boo was kinda cute," Britt said as they made it to Bama's crib.

"You know Savage would kill both of y'all," Big D said with a chuckle.

"Savage is just a friend, not my man, so mind your fucking business," Britt said with anger in her voice.

Britt never knocked when she went in Bama's crib. He was like her brother, and Mr. Curt was like a father to her. Britt and Big D walked into the crib to hear Future's album blasting from the stereo. What Britt saw next had her little panties wet.

Bama and Savage were exercising in the living room. Savage had his shirt off doing pushups and curling 50-pound dumbbells while sweat was dripping off of his chiseled eight pack. Savage had the body of a full-grown man, and a god, which turned all the females on, even grown women.

"You going to stare, sis, or give me a hug?" Savage asked Britt. She looked lost. All she could do was blush and hug him. Big D shook his head and went straight to the refrigerator to get a snack because Big Curt always kept snacks. Shit, what person close to 400 pounds didn't keep snacks?

"Guess who I just saw laying dead up the street," Big D said, once everybody was sitting down, listening to music.

"Who? Nigga, this ain't a guessing game," Bama said as he turned the music down after his last set of pushups.

"That nigga Boo, somebody did that nigga dirty, all head shots," Big D said, eating oatmeal pies.

"It's about to be a war. I'm glad we not into that type of shit," Britt said as she kicked off her Air Max 95 shoes. Big D shook his head in agreement with her.

"Y'all scared?" Savage said.

"Naw, nigga, I ain't never that. Niggas die every day, B. He'll be alright," Big D said in a New York accent, trying to sound like Cam'ron from the movie *Paid in Full*.

Bama looked at Savage, knowing he killed Boo. *He could have at least told me that*, he thought to himself. Bama wondered how a person could be so calm and relaxed after killing another person.

Savage put on his t-shirt and walked to the back, leaving everybody in the living room. Two minutes later, Savage walked back into the living room with three heavy duffle bags. This caught everybody's attention.

"Can I truest everybody in here?" Savage said as he dropped the bags on the couches.

Britt and Big D said "yeah" in unison.

"This was all Boo's shit. Now it's ours," Savage said as he poured the money, drugs, and guns onto the couches.

Big D and Britt's eyes grew wide with shock. No words could express their feelings, but Britt was used to drugs, money, and guns. Her brother was a kingpin in Miami.

"MPM and Zoe Pound had Miami on lock for years. Shit, they still do, but it's our time," Savage said with a smile. "If anybody is scared, or not sure, you can still leave because it's about be a World War III out here," Savage added.

Everybody stayed seated, so that was all Savage needed to see.

"Everybody take a gun. We gonna split the money and wholesale the drugs, and hopefully, by time we're done, we'll find a new connect," Savage said.

"Big D can split everything, just leave my half here. I'm about to plan some parties," Savage said before he left Bama's crib with two new guns on him. He'd already thrown the murder weapon away.

Chapter 18

The Plan

Two weeks passed. Word was spreading like wildfire about what had happened to Boo. Pole and the MPM crew didn't take the news well at all, so they put a $20k bounty on Boo's killer.

Savage decided to go to school, just keep his mom off his back and to lay low. The money was coming fast. The onions Savage was selling were moving like hot cakes. Savage knew education was important, too many blacks were uneducated. Savage wanted more than a street life, or to end up dead or in prison before he was 18, like most teens he knew.

Savage had heard the rumors going around school, and in the streets, about the manhunt for Boo's killer. The school was packed with loud ass teens walking the dirty hallway. Savage was getting his science book out of his locker for his science class. Britt approached Savage looking sexy in her tight red mini skirt and Jimmy Choo high heels. Britt was 16 but she had the body and curves of a grown woman, which made any man do a double take.

Savage looked Britt up and down. "Damn, Britt, you look nice. Why you all dressed up?" Savage asked, still focused on her body.

"Glad you like it," Britt said, smiling at his reaction.

Savage noticed a mark under Britt's left eye, even though she tried to hide it under the makeup. Once Britt saw Savage staring at her bruise, she tried to walk away, but he grabbed her arm.

Savage knew Louis put the mark under her eye because Britt told him she had to stay with him until JoJo came back from his business trip to New York. Savage realized every time she stayed with Louis, she would have bruises all over her body. He knew she was hurting.

Louis used to get drunk and hit her. He'd even grope her in her sleep, and she had no choice but to put up with it. Last night, she woke up to feel his finger in her virgin pussy. Britt fought back, only to receive a black eye.

One day, JoJo caught Louis hitting Britt and he'd almost beat him to death. After that, Louis put an order of protection on JoJo. That still didn't stop him from sending Britt there to stay a couple days when he went out of town.

Savage slammed his locker after he released her arm. "I swear to Allah, Britt, if he hit you again, I'm gonna kill him," Savage said as he walked away.

Britt stood there while Savage walked away because she knew he was mad, and serious. She could only hope Louis wouldn't try anything stupid, for the sake of his life.

At lunchtime, the cafeteria was like a fashion show, and gossip land, for students. Savage was sitting at the table planning his next move, while eating a cheeseburger. Jada approached the table, wearing a sundress.

"I like your Polo outfit," Jada said as she took a seat next to Savage.

"Thanks," Savage said, not even looking at her.

"Everybody around here is still talking about Boo's death and how his brother is going crazy," Jada said.

"So, that's life. People live and die," Savage said.

"Yeah, that's true, but I feel sad for his sister, Tiff. She was a close friend. She invited me to the funeral this weekend," Jada said. "Savage, I am always gone be here for you, but I kinda, umm." Jada's words were cut short when Britt and her friend, Tia, walked up to sit down with Savage.

Jada knew it was time to go because she knew both of the girls hated her, so she made her way to her next class. As she walked out of the cafeteria, she saw Bama walking in, looking fly with some Ray Ban glasses.

"Hey, Jada, where you going?" Bama asked.

"Class," Jada said as she walked faster to get away from Bama.

"What you doing this weekend? I'm trying to hit that," Bama said with a smirk on his face.

"Naw, I'm good. I have a bible study," Jada said, before speed walking away with her heavy backpack.

Bama was mad because she had some good, wet pussy, but he knew who she really wanted. *But fuck it,* he thought as he walked up to the crew.

"Why was she here?" Britt asked Savage with an evil and jealous look in her eyes.

"What? Ain't it a free country?" Savage asked. "Plus, she just helped me plan my next move, so everybody meet me at the spot Saturday morning," Savage said, before getting up to leave.

***

Savage left school in a cab that he'd called to take him to the mosque so he could make his Jummah prayer.

Savage arrived at the mosque around 12:30pm. He made his two Ra'kaats and sat down to listen to the Iman give his speech about Qur'an and Islamic issues in society.

"Fighting in the wrong things," the Iman said in his stern voice. "We fight for drugs, money, and girls, but we can fight mentally and physically for Allah," the Iman added.

The Iman continued to speak about drugs, violence, and murders.

Savage prayed for forgiveness for his sins, and the sins he was about to commit, and for all the bodies that was about to drop in Dade County.

Chapter 19

Funeral

Saturday morning, the crew waited in Bama's crib for Savage. Britt continued to check her watch, wondering where the fuck Savage was and why he'd told everybody to dress in all black Dickie suits.

"Why the long faces?" Savage said, looking around the room at everybody's ice grills.

"Maybe it's because you fucking late, and I'm on my period. And what the fuck is this meeting about?" Britt asked with an attitude.

Savage wanted to reply to her slick ass mouth, but he just ignored her and dropped the bags on the kitchen table. Big D's fat ass wasted no time grabbing a Wendy's bag and downing a burger and fries.

"Let's get down to business," Savage said.

"Bama, I need you to find a team of loyal soldiers that's down to kill and get money," Savage said. Bama shook his head, knowing who he was going to holla at because he knew a lot of young guns that wanted to be a part of something.

"Britt, I need you to tell your brother JoJo we need a connect so we can re-up a fill the streets with dope. We got money," Savage said, looking into Britt's green eyes.

"Big D, I need you to take care of all the money transactions, basically our account and our driver on missions," Savage said.

Big D just nodded his head as he ate the Wendy's, but he felt left out because he wanted to be about the action. Big D knew he wasn't a street nigga. He was a schoolboy and a football player, but he wanted to prove his loyalty.

"Today will change our lives because we're going to kidnap Pole as soon as Boo's casket drops," Savage said.

Britt and Bama acted as if they didn't care, but Big D's face said it all.

"How the hell are we going to kidnap him with his crew and family members around?" Big D asked, hoping he made sense so Savage would change his mind.

"That's why you're going to follow him, and when the time is right, we going to hop out, nigga," Savage said.

Big D swallowed so hard he almost choked.

"I hope everybody's ready. The stolen van is outside, and I'm sure everybody's strapped, too, so let's murk these niggas," Savage said with a wicked smile.

***

Pole was so upset he'd let his little brother fall victim to the streets. He knew he wasn't a street nigga. The thought of his little brother pressed his mind daily, and today was his funeral. Pole didn't want any of his MPM crew around while he figured all this shit out. He felt it could have been one of them,

Pole and his younger sister, Tiffany, were on their way out of the mini mansion headed to the funeral. Pole hopped in his black Jaguar while Tiffany hopped in her red Benz. Pole had already paid a security team to guard his mansion, just until shit cooled down.

Pole had recruited the grimiest killers and robbers in Miami to form MPM, but he couldn't trust his own soldiers. It was a cold game. Forty minutes later, they pulled up at the funeral, both looking like models, which made people's heads turn like owls.

Tiffany was seventeen years old with a body like Tyra Banks. She was light skinned with hazel eyes, long curly hair, and beautiful white teeth. Pole was her twin. He was light skinned with hazel eyes, long braids, and smooth skin. The ladies would do anything to get his attention, just so they could say they fucked the prince of Miami. Rumors had it that Pole and Trina had something going on, as well as the singer Mya.

Mostly everybody that was present at Boo's funeral were family members, friends, thots, and nosy ass muthafuckers that just wanted to see drama. As soon as Tiff and Pole approached their brother's casket, they broke down, because it was a closed casket. The doctor said there was no way to restore Boo's face. Even plastic surgery couldn't bring him look normal. So they had to settle for a closed casket funeral.

Pole and Tiff were crying, screaming, and unable to deal with the reality of life. After grieving, they took their seats by their Aunt Rosey and listened to the pastor speak to the crowd.

Pastor Jackson gave a long speech on behalf of Boo, saying how much of a good lad he was. Truth be told, the pastor didn't even know Boo, and he couldn't have cared less about the dead man. He just wanted to get it over with so he could go get drunk and buy some pussy.

Pole was so focused on his brother's picture that he didn't hear a word the pastor said. Pole swore to himself that he would find his brother's killer and punish him ten times worse than his little brother was.

Chapter 20

Youngin at Work

Young Goon was waiting near a car after some MPM members dropped him off because he wasn't into funerals, unless he was putting a nigga in a casket. Goon was eighteen years old, but his body count was over twenty-one. That's why the streets feared the young killer.

Growing up, Young Goon lived in Carol City, in a crack house, with his mother and her boyfriend, who was abusive. One late night, he and his little sister saw their mother getting beaten and they tried to help her. Charles felt little kicks to his legs, which caused him to stop beating Michelle and beat on Young Goon and his sister. With one closed fist to Young Goon's head, he passed out. Charles threw his sister, Monica, down the stairs, killing her instantly on impact.

Young Goon woke up to see his sister downstairs, not moving, with a twisted neck. Young Goon became enraged. He grabbed a big knife from the kitchen sink and ran towards Charles, who was so busy beating the life out of Michelle that he didn't feel the sharp pains in his back. He was stabbed in his neck and back over ten times, killing him where he stood.

Young Goon's mother was beaten so badly that she didn't make it either. She died from a broken neck and head trauma. Goon was placed in a mental hospital unit he turned 15 years old, then he ran away to live a street life.

***

Pole couldn't stay at the funeral any longer, so he told the MPM crew posted in the back to make sure Tiff got home safely, and made his exit. Pole made it to his car to see Goon in deep thought, as always. He'd basically raised him, so he knew him inside out.

"Come on, bruh, let's get the fuck outta here," Pole said as he hopped in his Jag, looking over his shoulder. Neither one of them noticed the black van tailing them as they pulled off.

Savage, Bama, Britt, and Big D pulled off slowly in the all-black van with ski masks on their faces and their guns cocked.

"I wonder who did this shit," Goon said.

"You ain't trying to send us a message," Pole said as he pulled off into traffic.

Goon just nodded his head. "The only nigga out here killing and trappin' is Zoe Pound, Top B, and the Cubans, but we don't deal with them at all," Good said.

"I don't know, but we need to find out," Pole said.

"I got killers. Bootz and the crew on it now, as we speak," Goon replied. "We on it, Blood, the wolves is out," Good continued, referencing the fact that most of the members of their crew were Bloods. Even Pole and Goon were gangbangers.

As they cruised through traffic, they pulled up behind an 18-wheeler at a red light. At the drop of a dime, a black van pulled up behind the black Jaguar, blocking the car in. Pole and Goon were caught up in their thoughts and unaware of the trap. Three masked men hopped out with big assault rifles pointed at the car.

"Don't fucking move, fuck boy, or I'm leaving your brains on the dashboard," Savage said, pointing an AK to Pole's head. Britt had Goon at gunpoint while Bama help Savage snatch Pole out of the car. Goon thought about reaching for his gun as he saw his friend being dragged in the street.

"Nigga, I wish you would," Britt said in a feminine voice as she read his mind.

"You going to be a dead bitch," Goon said with a smirk.

Savage and Bama tossed Pole in the van like a rag doll. Bama started pistol whipping him until he was unconscious. Savage was surprised the traffic light was still red as he made his way towards Goon. Goon was ice grilling Savage.

"I would let you talk shit, but it's too late," Savage said as he pointed his rifle toward Goon's head.

"Hold on," Britt said as she lowered Savage's gun. Goon looked confused, wishing they would hurry so he could meet the devil.

"This is how much I love you," Britt said stonily as she blew Goon away.

Chapter 21

Love and Death

"This is channel seven afternoon news. Hey, I'm Lara Patts reporting live from North Miami. As you can see, there was a murder at this stop light between Main and North Blvd," the news anchor said, pointing at the police surrounding Pole's car with yellow tape. The cameras turned towards the ambulance and EMS workers wrapping a dead body in white sheets.

"Witnesses say they saw three masked men hop out of an all-black van with big guns and murder one man," the reporter said. "I just received information announcing the murder victim was James Mattis, aka Goon, a well-known Blood gang member who was wanted for three homicides from New Jersey to Atlanta," the reporter stated.

"Also, we received information stating there was another victim at the scene, who was kidnapped, but police will not give any further information because the FBI is already investigating these victims," the reporter continued. "If you have any information, please contact 1-800-CRIME. This is Lara Patts reporting live from Miami, back to you John."

Bama and Savage sat in an abandoned apartment staring at the plasma TV in deep thought. Pole was in the next room, tied to a chair, duct-taped and barely alive, but breathing. Big D stood at the door with a Mack 11, waiting for a nigga to try to save a hoe. JoJo let Britt use his abandoned building, since he owned it. But he took people there to torture them, so Savage couldn't figure out why Britt wanted to chill there.

Savage walked into the cold room with boarded up windows to see Pole sleeping. Savage smacked Pole so hard with the 9mm Pistol that he wished he was dead.

Savage smelled shit, and from the look on Pole's face, he'd done it.

"Listen, bruh bruh, I'ma only ask you one fucking time. Where is the bands and dope? Any games, and your little sister, Tiff, will pay after seven soldiers run up in her," Savage said. Pole was shocked at how much this little nigga had done his homework on him. He had no choice but to respect his gangsta.

"Please don't hurt her. I'll give you everything, but most of it is in Jacksonville," Pole said with a swollen face.

Pole gave him the address, safe location, and codes.

"So, you're the Savage I heard about. Where is your big crew?" Pole asked.

Savage laughed, "Yeah, nice to meet you, Ms. Pole, or Ms. Steward," said Savage, calling him by his last name.

Pole closed his eyes and prayed Savage would spare him, but he saw a look in his eyes he'd never seen before that scared him.

Across town, Britt was riding back from burning the van in the woods behind an old Cuban restaurant. Britt had called JoJo to pick her up. JoJo had no idea why Britt was on that side of town when he thought she was at the abandoned apartment.

JoJo was bopping to his friend Gunplay's new album in his all-white Bentley when Britt turned down the volume.

"What the hell is wrong with you? Don't ever touch a gangsta's radio," said JoJo.

"I need a favor," Britt announced.

"I just did you two favors in one day by driving out here, and letting you and your friend use my spot," JoJo said, looking at her.

Okay, but this is real. It's for Savage. He is getting a lot of money, but he doesn't have a connect," Britt said.

"So how is he getting work?" JoJo asked.

Britt shrugged her shoulders. "He's my best friend and he don't fuck with nobody, but he is about his money. So I thought why not ask my big brother," Britt said, smiling.

JoJo thought for a second. He did like Savage, but he wondered if he could really be a plus to his million dollar business. JoJo thought about all the rumors he'd heard about young kids getting money and robbing major hustlers. *Could it be Savage?* He thought. Then he realized Britt was in his circle and he exited that thought.

JoJo was thirty-five years old and had never been to jail or even a police station, but yet he was a known killer and kingpin in Miami.

"Britt, I am going to do you a favor because I know you like the kid, but I know he's a hothead. This is the big boy league. Tell him he has to be consistent because I am a business man, and I conduct my time and product as I should," JoJo said.

"Tell him to meet me at my apartment downtown Monday afternoon because I know he don't go to school," JoJo said. And then added, "I know your ass better be going."

"Come on, bro, I'm about to graduate soon. I got this," Britt said as she turned up the volume, cutting off JoJo's speech.

Britt turned the music down again and JoJo continued, "Yeah, I need you to return the Range Tuesday because I need to get on..."

Britt cut him off by turning up the volume again, making him laugh at his little sister.

***

An hour later, Britt was in the abandoned building wondering why her hand was still numb from the shooting. Britt saw Big D watching TV but she walked past him and into the room Savage was in. Britt walked in to see Bama and Savage beating the shit out of Pole. They beat him so bad that he, looked like his face could be mountain climbed.

"Savage, could I talk to you?" Britt asked.

"Yeah, here I come," Savage said, putting on his shirt as if he'd been working out. "Bama, get ready to go out with Britt to get that money. The first stop is on the way to Jacksonville," Savage said.

When they walked back into the living room, Big D was nowhere in sight.

"What's up, Britt?" said Savage.

"Uhh, I spoke to JoJo and he said he'll fuck with you. So on Monday, you can meet him downtown in his apartment," said Britt.

"Wow, Britt, thanks. We on now," Savage said with a bright smile.

Savage felt something was wrong. "About earlier, you ain't have to do that. I'ma always protect you," Savage said.

Before he could finish, Britt cut him off. "I did that out of love," Britt said, as they stood face to face. "Savage, I want to be your wife, girl, lover, and best friend. I want you, but you have to take it slow, Randall, because I'm in love," she stated as a tear fell down from her green eyes.

Savage wiped her tears away. He felt the same way, but he never had a chance to express it, out of fear.

"So, you know what this means now, loyalty over death," Savage said with a serious look.

Britt nodded her head.

"So you're all mines now?" Savage asked, but before she could say yes, Savage was kissing her.

Bama walked out of the back room and saw them kissing. He was a little shocked.

"You ready, Britt?" Bama asked, breaking the passionate kiss.

"Yeah, let's go," Britt responded. She rushed out, grabbing her gun and the key to JoJo's Range.

Once they made it to the stash houses, they collected all of the guns, money, and drugs. Then they called Savage to confirm it was all good.

"Good news, Pole, everything checked out, but you gotta check in to hell," Savage said, walking towards Big D and handing him his gun. "You ready, Big D?" asked Savage.

Big D was nervous but he knew it was now or never. This was his opportunity to prove his loyalty. Big D walked up to Pole and looked him in his swollen eyes. Then he shot two rounds out of his Mack 11 into Pole's body.

Savage saw a menacing look in Big D's eyes that he'd never seen before. It made him feel a little uneasy, but he brushed it off.

Chapter 22

School ain't for me

Monday morning came around quickly. Savage woke up around 6am, ready to get money and put on for his crew. Savage thought about going to school, but as fast as that idea came, it left. Savage managed to get out of his bed. As he looked in his mirror, he smiled. "I'ma take it to the streets. Sleep is the cousin of death," Savage repeated to himself.

Savage dressed up in a pair of denim G Star jeans and a red Polo shirt, with some fresh J's. Savage walked into the kitchen after brushing his teeth He smelled eggs, turkey, pancakes, and hash browns.

"Damn, mommy, it smells good," Savage said as he took a seat.

"I know it do, baby. Mommy misses you, so I wanted to cook you breakfast," Lisa said. Savage knew this was his mom's way of trying to figure out where he'd been lately.

"I been at Britt and Bama's houses, studying for the exams coming up soon," Savage said.

Lisa gave him a sour look because she knew he was lying. The school had called over 30 times about his absences.

"Me and Britt been working on our relationship," Savage said, catching Lisa off guard.

"Tell mommy the juicy scoop," Lisa replied as she brought the plates to the table.

After talking about Britt for about twenty minutes, Savage knew she was for him.

"I know you liked that girl since you were a kid. Y'all always fought," Lisa said. "I just hope she don't take my baby from me," Lisa added with a frown.

"Man, can't nobody take me from you, except Allah. You will be my first and my last." Savage paused and then changed the subject. "I've been waiting to ask you why you have been so joyful," Savage asked.

"Well, if you must know, I met someone. We've been talking and dating," Lisa said as she put the empty dishes in the sink. "Nobody will ever make me happy as your father did. Even though he got my best friend pregnant, I still loved him dearly," Lisa said as she dazed off.

Savage changed the touchy subject because he saw his mom getting sad. "Where is he from and do he got kids?" Savage asked.

"He is from Miami. And yeah, he got three kids, but two were murdered. So he is an emotional wreck, but I am there for him," Lisa answered.

Savage just shook his head because niggas died every day in the 305. Savage was about to walk out as his mom cleaned the kitchen.

"Randall, do me a favor. Please stay safe in them streets. I know you're in them, because your dad was," Lisa said, looking him in the eyes.

"Yes, ma'am," Savage said as he walked out of the house.

***

Once outside, Savage called Britt. "Good morning, baby. What you doing?" Britt said as soon as she answered her phone.

"Nothing, just missing you," Savage said. "Oh yea? Good. So that means you'll be staying away from that bucktooth bitch Jada, because I know she in love with you," Britt said. "The bitch always posting shit up on social media and making indirect comments like I'm dumb," Britt added.

Savage didn't want to hear that. Jada was his last worry, but he knew it was deeper than him.

"Okay, baby," Savage said.

"I have to get to school, so I'll call you at lunch, baby. Go meet JoJo," Britt said.

"Okay, boo, but Jada means no harm. We grew up with her," Savage said with a frown.

"Yeah, but I do," Britt said as she hung up.

Savage walked to Bama's crib in deep thought. Three minutes later, Savage arrived at Bama's crib. As he made it to the porch, he thought about copping a car because he was out of breath. Savage saw Big Curt's big Yukon truck parked on the grass of the yard, so he knew his fat ass was home. As he rang the doorbell three times, he heard a deep voice say hold on.

Big Curt opened the door with food stains on his size 7X white tee.

"Stop pushing my damn doorbell, hoodlums," said Big Curt as he stared Savage up and down.

"Maybe, Mr. Curt," Savage said with a grin.

"Why you not a school? I hope you're not a drop out, like that little piece of shit in the room. Lisa would be pissed," Curt said as he walked into the living room to sit in his lazy boy. "No, Mr. Curt, I'm just taking some time off, but I see you losing weight," Savage said, making small talk.

"Oh yeah, I been running lately, and I lost over sixty pounds in a month," Curt said, lying his ass off.

"Soon you will be able to wear some skinny jeans," Savage said as he made his way to Bama's room.

As soon as Savage walked into his room, he saw Bama reading a Malcom X book. Bama was so into the book that he didn't even see Savage walk in. Savage pulled out a .357 gun as he creeped up behind Bama.

"Don't do it," Bama said as he pulled out a Colt 45 from under his lap.

"I'm never lacking, always packing and clapping," Bama said with a smile.

Savage laughed at his friend's statement. "Why you reading Malcolm X?"

"Because he was a strong, powerful leader to the black community," Bama replied.

"He was a street nigga, just like us, even a pimp before he changed his ways," Savage countered. "Anyways, where that paper at, folk? I'm about to go meet JoJo and I don't want shit on consignment," Savage said.

"That's real because we got it out the mud, bro," Bama said as he handed him two book bags full of blue faces. "Big D counted everything last night and we got a couple of pounds, one kilo, and over 250k left," Bama said, rubbing his ashy hands.

"Ok, sell the rest of that shit wholesale and get a couple of young hitters that want to get money and put them on," Savage said. "I'ma pull up when I get back and call a meeting with everybody. Have them here when I get back so we can put our plans together," Savage said as he left.

Chapter 23

Connect JoJo

North/Downtown Miami

Savage took a cab to the address Britt had given him, which was a nice condo built for the rich. Once he paid the miserable cab driver, he walked through the shiny lobby to the elevator to meet JoJo. He walked to apartment 3A with sweaty hands. He'd heard a lot about the kingpin, JoJo, but he understood business was business, no cuts.

He rang the bell and tapped the .357 on his waist to make sure it was steady, just in case shit went left. He trusted nobody.

"One second," a voice yelled.

JoJo opened the door in a Givenchy suit, looking Savage up and down, wondering who dressed him.

"Have a seat, Savage. You want a drink?" JoJo said as he walked to his large bar area.

"No, thank you," Savage said as he took a seat, looking around at the huge condo with a mink rug, artwork, classical paintings and wallpaper, and a view of the downtown area and North Miami.

"Good. A man should never drink on business meetings," JoJo said, taking a sip of white Henny he'd gotten from the Dominican Republic. I hear you trying to get money. Are you sure you ready for the good and bad of the game? The losses, the envy, the hate, the murder rate, the jail time?" JoJo asked.

"If I wasn't, I wouldn't be here. I love blood money," Savage said seriously, making JoJo laugh.

"Okay, look, I'm going to take a risk on you for two reasons. One is because my sister got love for you, and that's rare. She got a pic of you on her wall. And two is because I always got my ears to the streets, and your name is buzzing," JoJo said as Savage nodded his head. He was still shocked that Britt had a pic of him on her wall.

"I only have two rules so listen close. Don't fuck with my family or my money," JoJo said coldly.

"Respect. Business is never personal," Savage said.

"True, but it can get personal," JoJo replied with a dark stare, letting him know this was the real deal. "I am selling you keys for 15k and giving consignment. The work is good," JoJo said.

"No, I don't want consignment. I want to pay my way in the game," Savage said as he stacked $200,000 on the glass table, knocking down glass chess pieces.

JoJo looked at the money and smiled, already liking the young goon.

Savage left in a cab with a small green duffle bag, containing fifteen bricks of fish scale cocaine, and a big smile.

Chapter 24

The New Family

Porky Projects

Killer was next up in charge of running Miami since Pole's body was found chopped up into small pieces, in a public park, on a slide.

Killer's real name was Kiahiem. He'd grown up in Palm Beach with his aunty, who'd raised him from a young age because her sister, well stepsister, was found dead in a dope house in New York due to an overdose. Killer later moved to Miami with a cousin and started to get in trouble daily, which landed him in juvenile detention, where he met Pole.

The two became Bloods and best friends while still in jail. When Pole got out, MPM started and took over the streets. And when Killer came home, Pole took care of him. Killer was his shooter, but Pole had no clue that he was fucking Tiff and had taken her v-card.

He pulled up in his 96 Impala sitting on 28 inches with red paint. There were thirty MPM members posted up at their private headquarters, where they threw parties. It was a small house with a fence, and ten pit bulls in the back.

Once everybody entered the house, Killer took control.

"I need to address some shit, blood. We lost Boo, Pole, Goon, Bobby, and Blood Batti in less than 90 days. We getting robbed. This shit ain't how we get down, blood. I want to find out every nigga who moving weight in Miami. Then I'ma do my research. But keep getting money, blood. Piru for life. We MPM. I got the best plug. I've been supplying the family for years. We run Miami. Anybody get in our way, then we eliminate them. I'm out. Let's run up a check," Killer said as he went out back to watch a dog fight he had 50k on.

***

Meanwhile, across town, over twenty-five young teens sat in Bama's crib, staring at Savage as if was Jesus.

"Thanks for coming, but if a nigga ain't ready to kill or get money, they need to go because we play with them poles around here," Savage stated. Nobody left.

"Good. Now the only way out is death," Savage said while Big D rubbed his AK-47 like a cat.

"We about to take over Miami. All of you got a different area in Miami, and your our crew, but I have four rules: 1) No snitching, 2) stay strapped, 3) live with honor, 4) gain loyalty for each other, because we the youngins in charge," Savage stated.

"Fresh and Lil Shooter are the ones you will report to when you need to re-up and drop off, which will happen mainly every Friday," Britt stated.

"Does anybody have any concerns or questions?" Savage asked. "Ok, good. I got a half of key for everybody in here, and a couple of racks for your pockets," Savage said before he left with Britt.

Chapter 25

Get Money Clique

Savage woke up just in time for his Fajr prayer. He'd had a hard time sleeping. He couldn't stop thinking about the MPM niggas he was at war with. He went in the bathroom. Then he made his prayer and read his Nobel Qur'an.

He had plans to take his GED because school was out of the question for him. He'd called Britt the previous night and told her his plan, and she went crazy on him. Savage had plans to be Richard Porter, Big Meech, or Guy Fisher before imprisonment.

***

Carol City

Savage's crew was in full effect in Carol City's most dangerous project. It was called The Hole because there was only one way in and one way out.

Fresh controlled the projects, which looked like the black cartel.

"Yo, Fresh, I need two onions, bruh. Shit is fire," an older drug dealer/fiend, named Big Fred, asked Fresh.

"You lucky I'm almost out," he said, sliding him an onion of crack, aka ounce. Fresh had sold a brick in a couple of hours.

"Nino Brown ain't got shit on me," Fresh yelled from the playground area in his project.

Fresh's hood was hot with police. They circled the hood every ten minutes when they weren't hopping out on niggas. That is why he gave young niggas packs. Police never fucked with little kids.

Fresh's older brother had taught him the game before he was murdered outside his side bitch's crib. Fresh had vowed to kill his brother's murderer's whole family one day. This particular night was a party night. All the work was gone and the goons wanted to turn up in the city. So it was Fresh's treat.

***

O-Town

Lil Shooter was posted on the block with a gang of dread head Haitians. This was his hood. Lil Shooter was born in Compton, CA, and raised in Jacksonville and Miami, so he had an army all over. Not to mention, he was a Hoover Crip, but Miami didn't gangbang, they hood banged.

His mom was in prison and his father had been gunned down by a blood in LA years before he moved to Florida.

Lil Shooter was out of work. He planned to go clubbing with Fresh. He loved to have fun, standing on the block wasn't his style.

Chapter 26

B-Day Surprise

Savage's 18th birthday was a month later and everything was going well. He'd had to re-up five times in a month. He was up now.

"What's good for tonight, bruh? It's my big day," Savage said, sitting on his new all-white AMG Benz Coupe as he chilled with Bama in front of his crib.

"The K.O.D. going to be litty. We throwing you a big party, but don't tell nobody I told you. Britt set it up," Bama said, pouring lean into a Sprite bottle. Savage wasn't heavy on drugs or alcohol, but his birthday was a different story.

"I won't tell her. She studying for some test."

"Bruh, on some real gangsta shit, Britt more G'd up than any of us. It's something in her eyes. It's like its two Britts," Bama said, making him laugh.

"I'ma go get ready for tonight. I gotta park the Benz at Ms. Jackson's crib. My neighbors be nosey, hate to see a young nigga getting money," Savage said as he pulled off, on his way to his mom's crib.

***

Savage walked to his house after he'd parked two houses up the block in Ms. Jackson's driveway. She was like family.

It was a happy day, but also a sad day. It was Savage's 18th birthday but also marked eighteen years since his father's murder, and the killer was still somewhere lurking.

Savage wondered why the house lights were off and his mom's car was in the driveway. He felt something was off. He slid his 44mag from his waist and held it to his side as he used his key to open the door.

"Surprise," everybody yelled, scaring him, but almost getting them all shot.

Lisa gave her son a hug as well as friends and family. Britt jumped in his arms, kissing his soft lips. She looked beautiful in her sundress and heels.

Bama and Jada walked into the house, joining the party.

"She told me to tell you happy b-day, bruh. Britt didn't want me to tell you about this surprise party," Bama said.

"I saw you tailing me, nigga. But you disappeared on Jada's block," he replied, letting him know he was on point.

"Happy Birthday, Savage," Jada said, giving him a light hug. Britt started to cough as she ice grilled Jada, letting her know her time was up.

"Thanks for pulling up," Savage said as he noticed an older, light skinned nigga in the kitchen with his mom, laughing.

"Oh, Randall, perfect timing. This is my friend Rich, who I used to work with," Lisa said, introducing the two.

"Happy Birthday," Rich said as he extended his hand to Savage, who shook it lightly, not feeling his vibe.

"How do it feel to be 18? I remember when I was your age," Rich said.

"All that is cool, but just treat my mom as if she was your own," Savage said before walking off to mingle with the guests.

"Big D, you coming out tonight? I know the gang popping up," Bama said.

"Nigga, hell yeah. I'm trying to see some ass," Big D stated, looking at Jada, who sucked her teeth.

"Let me guess, you going too," Britt said, trying to trick Savage.

"Yeah, I'm going, but you coming too. If not, then I'm not going," he said, sounding honest.

"Shit, you damn right I'm going. Them bitches ain't got shit on me, and I'll be damned if you slide with a stripper. I know how y'all get down," Britt said, pointing to Lil Shooter and a crew of young goons playing XBOX.

Lisa brought out a big cake with candles. Britt whispered something in his ear that had him blushing as he made the same wish he'd been making for ten years, to find his dad's killer.

The crew chilled until it was time to go out clubbing.

Chapter 27

King of Diamonds

The MPM crew was ready to party. They were five cars deep, all in red BMW sedans, coupes, and trucks.

"Yoo, bruh, I had my ears to the streets, and word is there's a new clique of getting money niggas all over Miami," Bootz told Killer as they walked towards club KOD to enjoy themselves for the night.

"Do your homework on them fools, blood. If shit don't add up, we going to turn the city up," Killer said as they passed the long line outside.

***

Savage and his crew pulled up to the club looking like movie stars in Hollywood. Savage parked the all-white Bentley GT coupe, with the top back, in front of the club.

They weren't the only ones stunting. Bama pulled behind him in a sky blue Benz, E-class 300. Big D pulled up in an all-white M2 228i BMW on rims, with tints, while Fresh and Lil Shooter pulled up in two Cadillac trucks full of goons.

Savage and Britt walked into the club dressed in all white, as if it was a white affair party. Savage wore a white Gucci outfit. Britt wore an all-white Fendi dress, looking like a snack. The whole club stared at her, wondering if she was a dancer or a bottle girl.

The club was turned up, with loud music and strippers hanging from the ceiling doing gymnastic moves. There were TVs behind the bars. Money machines and money guns were posted next to every stage. The dancing lights made the club more appealing as the song Rack City turned the crowd up and money flooded the stages.

Once the crew made it to one of the VIP sections, the DJ shouted at Savage, wishing him a Happy Birthday.

"I hope these stanky bitches popping their roast beef pussy for me," Britt said with a laugh as a couple of strippers entered the VIP section twerking.

"Maybe so," Savage said as he told the beautiful bartender to bring ten bottles of Ace of Spades and ten bottles of Dom P.

The crew was all over the club, throwing money. They were twenty deep as Savage and Britt tossed 30K to the dancers in the VIP section. Savage had been feeling eyes on him ever since he walked in, and his vibes were right. There was another crew across the club in the other VIP section, ice grilling.

***

"Killer, who them niggas over there, tossing all that money? They shutting the club down. They must be from New York or ATL," one of Killer's soldiers stated.

Killer was thinking the same thing as dancers ran in and out of their VIP sections with arms full of money.

"I don't know, blood, but I'm not feeling it," Killer said.

"That's them niggas from O-Town. His name Fresh. He a little hitter. You remember his brother, Munchy, homie? They from the hole," Bootz said, not knowing anybody else over there, except Fresh.

Killer couldn't keep his eyes off the dude in the all-white and the bad light skin bitch with him. He stood out.

"Send them four bottles of Ace. Whoever they are, let's welcome them to my town," Killer told one of his goons, who yelled down a bottle girl.

***

"You know them niggas in the corner VIP section?" Savage said, whispering in Fresh's ear as he was getting a lap dance by a big booty Haitian chick named Rosey.

"Yeah, that's them MPM niggas. What's up? You want me to send them a message?" Fresh said, pushing the stripper off his lap and grabbing his 45 pistol with a glizzy 3 grand clip attached to it.

"Nah, let it play out. Enjoy yourself," Savage said as Britt slid her 380 special back in her Fendi purse. She was ready. The bartenders approached their section with two bottles with sparkles.

"Who order these?" Savage asked everybody over the music.

"I believe it's from the other VIP section," the dark brown skinned bottle girl said, pointing to the MPM niggas.

"Okay. Send them bottles back, and send them ten more. You can keep the change," Savage said, handing her close to 15k in cash, all blue faces. Her face lit up from the biggest tip she'd ever received.

"Thank you so much. Happy Birthday," she said, blushing.

"Have a good day. We will call you when we need you, ma," Britt said, seeing the girl was getting friendly with Savage. Britt could tell she was a sack chaser, like every other bitch in the club.

Minutes later, the bottle girls pushed a cart of Ace of Spades to the MPM crew. They denied the bottles and were pissed as they left the club with hate and envy in their hearts.

After partying, the crew all went different ways. Some went to other clubs, like Bama and Lil Shooter, while the rest of the crew went home or to the hotel with a couple of dancers.

As soon as Savage hit the expressway, he started to feel the champagne and Britt started to rub on his manhood.

"Drive to that hotel on Collins Ave," Britt told him. "I told you I got a big surprise for you," she said, licking her juicy lips as Savage got off on Exit 4, staring at her thick thighs.

Chapter 28

The First Time

Britt had already paid for the penthouse pad. It was large and beautiful. She'd paid two thousand dollars a night, but it was worth it. It had marble floors, glass vases, gold chandeliers, fur rugs, and the best view of Miami, of course.

"Dinner is on the balcony," she said as she took off her heels and walked to the balcony. Her ass bounced with every step because she took off her thong. Her body was thick in all the right places, and it was all natural.

The two sat down and stared at each other. Then they laughed. They always admired each other's beauty.

"Britt, this is nice. You ain't have to do this," he said, eating well cooked steak and looking at Miami's night life.

"Don't worry, it's only the beginning," she said with an evil grin. The both of them talked and laughed until it was bedtime.

"I'ma lay down. I had a live night," Savage said, getting up from the table.

After he kissed her, Britt rushed into the shower and put on the pink lingerie set from Chanel that showed her perky breast and phat, clean shaved pussy lips.

"Baby, wake up," Britt said, standing in front of Savage. He'd taken a quick nap, but he woke up immediately when she crawled between his legs.

"Britt, you a virgin. What the…" was all he could say before she cut him off.

"Not after tonight, please fuck me," she said, sucking his neck as he fingered her tight, wet pussy, and then licked his finger to taste cherries.

Savage wasted no time as he took control. He laid her on her back and slid off her panties to see a small, pretty, dripping wet pussy. He licked her small clit while fingering her. She grabbed his dreads, moaning.

Britt was in ecstasy, trying to hold back her screams and moans, but she couldn't.

"Ugh, I'm cumming," she yelled as she came hard, squirting all over the place, like a waterfall.

After her climax, they traded places. She saw his big dick and neatly trimmed hair and got wetter as she stroked his dick, licking the tip slowly. Britt sucked his dick slowly while messaging his balls. She did tongue tricks on his dick.

"Damn. Suck that shit," Savage moaned as she spit on his dick, going deeper until she felt it in the back of her throat, making her tear up.

Once she got the rhythm, she was able to deep throat the whole nine piece pipe like a pro. She relaxed her throat as he fucked her face. Savage couldn't hold on, he came in her mouth within seconds, while she kept sucking and slurping on his dick and cum. With one flip, Britt's legs were over his shoulders as he entered her tight, wet pussy.

"Ugh, shit, daddy," she moaned, biting her lips as he opened her up.

"You like it?" Savage gritted as he moved his hips deeper into her walls. She dug in his chiseled back, trying not to nut on his dick, but it was building up. Britt was on cloud nine as her eyes rolled up into her head. She couldn't believe the pleasure and pain she felt.

"Oh yea, fuck that pussy. Fuck me harder. Omg, babe, go deeperrr," she yelled, while he was hitting her G-spot. After they both came twice, he bent her over and fucked her doggie style like a champ, until she begged him to stop.

He wasn't done. He continued to fuck her. Once she was able to take the dick, she started throwing her ass back and twerking on his dick, until they came again.

When they were done, Savage saw red dots of blood all over the white sheets.

"I'm sorry," she said, embarrassed, forgetting he'd popped her cherry. The two cleaned up, took a shower together, and went for round two in the shower.

Chapter 29

After the Club

Killer and Tiff were in their house, going back and forth.

"Tiff, I been bossy with bills, death, and the streets. Babe, I'm here to protect and love you," Killer said. He got tired of hearing her complain every night.

"I know, but I never see you no more. I'm scared I'ma lose you to the streets, like my brothers," she said, as she laid in their bed, crying.

"Baby, I'm sorry. I will spend more time with you. Stop crying," he said, leaning into her and wiping her tears.

Tiff felt his dick print and smiled. She needed some dick, so she wasted no time in climbing under the sheets and sucking his dick like a lollipop. After slurping and deep throating her man for over ten minutes, he nutted in her mouth, while she played with his cum, getting nasty.

She was ready to fuck, so she bent over on all fours, showing her big clit and thin pussy lips. Killer went in slowly because Tiff couldn't take no dick, and he loved to see her run from it.

"Oh yes, fuck me, call me names, choke me," Tiff yelled as Killer long stroked her, making her climax back to back. He kept drilling her pussy from behind until he felt himself cumming. He nutted on her ass while she was shaking like a stripper, making it clap. Tiff was Lisa Raye's twin, but thicker, and her hair was real and longer. Tiff was drained she was ready to shower and sleep.

"I'ma go wash this kitty. You know how to give me some act right," she said, kissing the tip of his semi-soft dick that was hanging.

Killer laid in the bed, thinking about the crew of young niggas he'd seen. It was bothering him, but he knew, sooner or later, they would be exposed.

***

Bama and Big D were with two beautiful strippers from the club named, China and Bubbles. They were both down for whatever as long as the money was right.

"Can't no bitch suck a dick like me, baby," China said, diving deep on Big D's dick and sucking it at a fast speed, twisting her head like an owl, and making him want to cry.

Bama had Bubbles bent over on the living room floor, fucking her from behind as he slapped her ass.

"Yesss, fuck me. Put it in my ass. Ram it in, please," Bubbles begged, her light colored ass looking red.

Bama wasted no time ramming it in her asshole because her pussy was loose. He felt no grip, just wetness. When Big D was about to cum, he forced China's head deep down on his dick until she got all his kids down her throat, and she swallowed it like a pro. When Big D stood up, he almost lost his balance, her head game was so good.

"Damn, boy, you may need to do some squats," China said, fixing her hair. She was beautiful with Chinese features, chinky eyes, nice smile, and a dancer's body. But that wasn't why they called her China. It was because when she sucked dick, a nigga would speak Chinese, it was so good.

When Bama was done, he paid Bubbles and Big D paid China. Then they kicked them out. They wanted to stay but the guys were sick of them, and the house had a musky smell, thanks to Bubbles.

Big D and Bama played XBOX Call of Duty until the sun came up.

Chapter 30

Change

JoJo had just come back from a meeting with his connect, discussing business. His connect supplied most of the biggest drug lords in the south.

JoJo was being chauffeured around Miami in his all-white Maybach, thinking about all of his life achievements. Business had been great. Savage was running up a big bag, every trip, he would clean him out. So JoJo had plans to introduce him to his connect soon.

JoJo was planning on retiring from the game, but before he did, he wanted everything to be set. He'd built a strong empire, with the help of powerful men. He was very well connected.

He turned all his dirty money into clean money to keep the feds off his line. Life was great for JoJo as he stared at the palm trees, loving the beautiful view of his city, as the Maybach glided through the streets.

***

Savage and Britt took an early morning swim in the indoor pool, at the four-star hotel, before they plan to check out.

"I've been thinking, babe," Britt said with her southern voice as she climbed out of the pool in her off-white two-piece bikini, showing her curves.

"What?" he asked, looking into her bright green eyes.

"We should get our own house, or apartment, or townhouse, so we can focus on us. I'm sick of living with JoJo. He's always gone, and I want to be around you," she said sadly.

"Are you ready for that? You're still in school and you start college right after," Savage said, hoping to talk her out of it. "Plus, I'm in the field heavy. I want you to be safe."

"Nigga, I'ma ride or die bitch. I'm not trying hear that. I'ma gangsta, too. You seen my work," Britt said, standing between his legs with her arms across her breast.

"Britt, I want better for you. This life ain't…"

"Savage, I am a part of this fucking crew, just like you. So don't try to play me or question my loyalty," she yelled as she walked off, ass jiggling, and tears in her eyes.

"Hold up. It's not like that, Britt. Lighten up. I want you to be safe, period," he said as he caught up to her.

"Nigga, kiss my yellow ass, fuck outta here," she said, walking off with an attitude.

***

Savage made it home hours later. He'd dropped Britt off at home, and she'd said nothing to him at all.

He walked into his house to see Rich sitting in the living room, wearing his clothes, and watching ESPN sports center. Savage was pissed off.

"Yo, bruh, you lost your fucking mind? How did you get my pajamas?" Savage asked furiously.

Rich looked confused because he had no clue they was his clothes. They fit him perfectly. Lisa had given him the clothes that morning after they spent the night together.

"No disrespect, Randall, but Lisa gave them to me this morning because my clothes were soaked last night. They're still washing now," Rich said nonchalantly, in his defense.

"Naw, you in my crib. It's obvious you fucking my mother and now you wearing my clothes, fuck nigga?" Savage yelled, getting face to face with Rich, waiting for him to bust a move.

"I won't be too many fuck niggas," Rich said seriously.

"Bust your move, old nigga," Savage said.

Lisa heard all the commotion and came out from the back in her silk robe, covering her panties, flat stomach, and big, nice breasts.

"Randall, what the fuck is going on? Get out of that man's face," Lisa yelled.

"Man, why you got this nigga wearing my shit?" Savage yelled, pissed off.

"First, watch your damn mouth in my house. I'm grown. Don't question shit I do," Lisa demanded. "Rich is here with me. Respect it, or leave. You're eighteen now, pushing a damn Bentley, or whatever it is," she screamed, letting him know she wasn't dumb. Savage couldn't believe his ears. He'd never heard Lisa spazz out on him like this. Rich tried to calm her down because it wasn't that serious, but she wouldn't stop. She followed him to his room. "You're jeopardizing my home and career selling that poison. You should be ashamed of yourself," she yelled as he packed three small duffle bags full of money and clothes.

He left silently, without saying a word. He hopped in his Benz and pulled off, calling Britt, who wasn't picking up. Savage called one more time, and she picked up, half sleep with an attitude. He told her everything that had happened and how he wanted to get them a place. She happily agreed.

Chapter 31

Let's Play

Bootz was on a serious mission when he hopped in the Benz truck. "I'ma find out who them young niggas was with Fresh. This shit not adding up," Bootz said on his cell phone as he made his way to O-Town to research some shit.

Bootz was twenty-seven years old, born in VA, but raised in Dade County. He'd been down with MPM and his Piru blood set since he was in middle school, running around robbing niggas.

Twenty minutes later, the Benz truck pulled up in the hole. It was a big housing project that was supposed to have been shut down because it wasn't inhabitable. Bootz saw fiends running around everywhere, like it was New Jack City. He was shocked. He used to go down there regularly and he never imagined it becoming like this.

"Yo, shawty, let me holla at you, cuz," Bootz yelled out his window to a fiend, who was skipping down the block, ready to take his hit.

The fiend stopped and looked at the clean Benz, wondering who he knew that was in it.

"Listen, I need some shit. I'm not police or jack boy, I'm trying get high. I heard they got good shit out here," Bootz said as crackhead Dice saw dollar signs.

"Ok, I can help. But what's in it for me?" Dice said with no teeth in his mouth, only gums.

"Nigga, I got a hundred, but I need eighty worth, and you keep the rest," Bootz said as Dice looked at him as if he was crazy.

"I look like a crackhead to you? I want 50/50 or no play," Dice said, knowing Bootz was a crackhead now because he was playing fiend games.

"Ight, bruh, here," Bootz said as he handed the man a blue face before he ran off into one of the buildings.

Five minutes later, Dice came back smiling ear to ear, like a big kid, as he climbed in the Benz's passenger seat.

"I took my three twenties. Fresh always give me a deal because his crew got the city on lock. They took over out the blue. I'm telling you," Dice said as he climbed out, happy. He'd just given Boots three dimes that looked like 20s.

"Thank you. Have a safe trip," Bootz said, confusing Dice before he blew his skull on the hot pavement. Bootz pulled off as everybody watched the Benz with the MPM plates leave the hole.

***

Bama was in his kitchen, eating a bowl of Froot Loops cereal, watching a Malcolm X movie, and wondering why Malcom X never killed the nigga who had put the hit out on him. The phone ringing interrupted his thought process. Bama was heavy on Black Revolution Movements.

"Holla," Bama answered, pissed off.

"I'm about to pull up on you. We need to talk," Fresh said, hanging up, not taking no for an answer.

Bama looked at the phone and shook his head.

"Big D, that was Fresh, crying about some shit," Bama yelled to the back room of his crib where Big D was counting all the re-up money with money machines.

"Iight, I already know it's some damn shit, bruh. I got football practice. And why my dick hurt every time I piss, bruh? It feel like I'm pissing out nails, cuz. You ever felt that shit?" Big D said, scratching his dick.

"Hold on," Bama said, almost choking on his cereal. "Did you piss out some green shit, like the Hulk was in you?" Bama asked.

"Yeah. Yeah. How you know that, folk? I thought I had liquor poison," Big D stated as Bama started to laugh so hard that he was on the floor spinning around, dying.

"What's so funny?" Big D said.

"She burnt your damn ass," Bama said, still laughing while Big D ran in the back room to call Bubbles. Her phone went to voicemail each time.

***

"I'm telling you, Killer, them niggas moving weight, and they got good work. The fiends going crazy," Bootz said while he watched his workers bag crack and dope up throughout out the trap house. "It's no way they came up overnight. I think we found our guys. You said they moving work all around Miami, but for who, is my concern," Killer replied in deep thought.

"I don't know, but I'm going to find out, boss," Bootz stated seriously, ready to kill.

***

Fresh pulled up to Bama's crib with a GMC truck full of goons, ready for war, dressed in all black, with pistols. Fresh didn't even knock, he just invited himself into the crib. Luckily, Big Curt wasn't there or he would've gotten cursed out.

"Somebody came through my hood and killed a fiend, Dice was a legend in the hole. He killed 2 cops back in the day, and got acquitted," Fresh said, pacing in the living room.

"Nigga, that's what's so important, a fucking fiend?" Bama said.

It was them MPM niggas. A young bitch I be fucking told me she saw a Benz with MPM license plates leave the crime scene after he smacked the nigga. Bruh, they disrespected my hood. That was a message," Fresh said.

"Listen, stay strapped and shoot first, ask later, or never ask. Just stay on point. I'ma holla at the crew. And next time you come to my crib, knock first." Bama said as Fresh left, pissed off and ready to kill MPM members.

Chapter 32

Life is a Gamble

Weeks Later

Savage and Britt moved into a nice condo near South Beach. It was beautiful.

"This is so nice, baby. I'ma put a woman's touch on it, no worries," Britt said, looking around. They'd packed the apartment full of new shit.

"What we doing for my graduation?" Britt asked, emptying some boxes.

"It's up to you and Big D. I heard he got five college scholarships for football. You also got some good scholarships, babe. I'm proud of you," he told her as she kissed him and grabbed his dick.

"Baby, I want to fuck in the shower," she whispered in his ear. Lately, she'd been horny. They would fuck all day, anywhere. Since she lost her V card, she'd been going crazy.

"I'm not really in the mood, I need some sleep," he said, walking to their master bedroom. Britt knew something was wrong. She hated to see him stressed or sad. She went to take a shower and rubbed her clit until she climaxed in their glass shower with gold trim.

***

Carol City

"Fresh, that's one of them MPM traps right there, where all them blood niggas at," a young soldier from Carol City shouted from the backseat.

"Pull over, Rel," Fresh said as he saw niggas chilling on the block in front of a rundown crack house.

"Follow my lead," Fresh told his soldiers in the truck behind him through his walkie-talkie. Fresh hopped out with eight niggas, carrying assault rifles, and nobody saw them coming at full speed from across the street.

***

"Lil Moe, I got the fucking round, so put all bets on the floor, shawty, because you broke ass niggas still owe me," BA shouted in his deep New Orleans accent.

The trick dice landed on 4, 5, and 6 making the small crowd go crazy, as if they won the money.

"Give me my money, bitch nigga," BA shouted loudly. But before he could pick up his money, the butt of an AK busted his head, knocking him out.

"What the fuck?" Lil Moe yelled, scared to death when he saw all the masked men pointing assault rifles at all of them.

"Everybody fucking strip, now. And if you fucking make any funny move, I'ma send a dozen roses to your mom for you," Fresh said with a laugh, watching everybody strip ass naked.

"Y'all don't know who y'all fucking with. This MPM turf," Lil Moe said, speaking up, while covering his small dick with his hands. His name was little Moe for a reason.

"Okay, you must be the team captain. Give your boss a message for me, get down or lay down," Fresh said as he nodded his head to his crew. They killed all nine MPM members and walked off.

"You got a new chief in town, take note. My name Fresh," he yelled as they got back into their trucks to leave.

Shortly after the massacre, Killer received terrible news from Bootz, but he'd already seen it on the news. It was time for a meeting with every MPM member.

***

Two Hours Later

Killer walked into the packed warehouse he used to store car parts for his auto body shops. Everyone had their attention on Lil

118

Moe, who was in the front row, nervous. Bootz and Killer stood in the front, while everyone else sat down.

"Lil Moe, step up," Killer said, sternly, as if he was about receive a badge of honor. Lil Moe was Bootz blood cousin, but he couldn't even look at him.

"One question? Why you not dead, homie?" Killer asked.

Lil Moe thought it was a trick question, but he wasn't about gamble with his life.

"They told me they was sparing my life so I could deliver their message. I told them to kill me, but they laughed at me and killed the homies," Lil Moe said in a sad voice, thinking it would change his fate. Bootz and Killer looked at each other, wondering who was playing games.

"So you a mailman, now?" Killer yelled.

"No, sir," Lil Moe replied.

"What they say?" Killer asked.

"His name was Fresh. He told me to tell you to get down, or lay down," Lil Moe said nervously.

"Fuck," Bootz yelled as he kicked a chair across the warehouse.

"I'm sorry, I couldn't do nothing," Lil Moe told Bootz, who walked off.

"It's okay. Allah forgives, I don't," Killer told Lil Moe, who looked puzzled by his comment. Before he could say another word, Killer placed five bullets in his heart.

"Let this be my message to all you niggas, never leave a homie for dead and you alive," Killer said. "Find all them little niggas and kill their whole family. These are kids playing a grown man's game," Killer said before leaving to go home.

"Clean this bitch ass nigga up," Bootz said, as he thought of some story to tell his aunty when his cousin popped up missing.

Chapter 33

Graduation and Retirement Party

Savage walked into the five-star restaurant in an all-black Prada suit with his Stacey Adams, looking like money. JoJo was sitting in the back booth with an older gentleman he'd never seen before, but he could tell he was powerful.

After greeting both men with firm handshakes, Savage sat down at the end of the booth.

"OG, this is the young man I've been telling you about," JoJo said, smiling.

"I see. Nice to meet you, Savage. I heard a lot of good things about you," OG said with a warm smile, fixing his tie on his tailor-made suit.

"Likewise," Savage stated, as the food arrived.

They talked for over an hour about the government, economics, business, war or Isis, and future plans.

"Enough of the political shit because I know you can go all day. But as you know, I'm retiring soon, and I want to leave the game to Savage. I am passing the torch to him," JoJo said while Savage choked on his water.

OG knew he was about to lose a lot of money, but JoJo was like a son to him, so he was happy he was leaving the game alone. If it was anyone else, they would have been dead before midnight.

"I'm no longer the middleman. That's why I called this lunch," JoJo said, looking at them both.

"Okay, your wish is granted. I have a meeting in Texas. I have to hop on my private jet. Thank you for the lunch. Savage, here is my info. Hit me up Friday, sometime, so we can get up and further discuss business," OG said as he stood up to leave. OG was dark, in shape, and had waves. He reminded Savage of Keith Sweat, without the grey hair. After the meal, Savage was happy it went smoothly. Now he had a plug.

***

Graduation night was lit. The high school kids had a long day of long lectures from teachers and students.

JoJo's mansion was packed with teenagers, students, tycoons, gangstas, kingpins, and powerful people to show love to Britt, for graduating, and JoJo, for his retirement.

Britt wore a strapless pink Ferragamo dress, showing lots of skin and curves. Her hair was hanging down her back, and she had on a little makeup.

The backyard was popping with loud music, free food, liquor, games, and drugs. Most of the teens were too high or drunk to know where they were.

"Excuse me, can I have your attention? I'm JoJo, and this is Britt, my little sister that I'm very proud of. Thank you for coming out. I'm retiring, so this is my retirement party, as well as my beautiful sister's graduation party. To show her how proud I am of her, I have a gift for her," JoJo said, handing her a box.

"What's this?" Britt said as she opened it on stage, revealing a set of two keys.

"One key is for your pink Bentley coupe, out front, and the other key is a mansion, two blocks down, paid in full," JoJo said on the mic, stunting, while Britt hugged him and the crowd got loud and crazy.

The DJ started the music again as the large crowd started dancing and females started twerking all over the stage.

***

Grapes and gold diggers were in motion all over the mansion, Big D and Bama had two chicks a piece, and they were ready to fuck.

"Let's go out tonight, I promised Savage and Britt," Big D told Bama, who wasn't trying to leave the two white bitches that were ready to fuck.

"Go with them. I'ma go across town. Plus, you still got that flu down there. I'm not sharing pussy with you," Bama said, laughing and walking off with two bad college bitches.

When it was time to go out, they all left in different cars. They were unaware of the trouble that lurked behind them.

***

Bootz was on their asses. He'd heard about the graduation from his little sister and her friends. Not to mention, Bootz had been on JoJo's line for years.

It wasn't hard to put together. Fresh's crew was turning the city up but all he'd heard of was Savage's crew, so it wasn't hard to figure out they were both connected to JoJo. Bootz promised himself that after this night, all his homies would be able to rest in peace.

Chapter 34

Caught Slipping

On the way to the club, Savage made a pit stop. Britt and Big D followed him to some apartments in South Miami, across the bridge. When Savage hopped out, they were wondering what the fuck he had going on.

"What's up folk? What's going on?" Big D said, hopping his big frame out of the Benz.

"Nothing, but you see this Bugatti?" Savage said, pointing at the most expensive luxury car in the city.

"That shit nice, but come on. We gotta go before somebody think we stealing their shit," Big D said as Britt chuckled.

"Congratulations, bro," Savage told Big D, handing him the keys.

"Ain't no way, bruh," Big D said as he climbed inside the deep racing seats.

"Thanks, bro, I know this is the both of your work, sis," he said, making Britt smile. They made their way to the club to enjoy the night, as if it was there last.

***

The VIP section in the club was popping. Everywhere you looked, bottles were being popped as partygoers enjoyed the dance music.

Big D had four women all to himself, while he sipped Ace of Spades. Britt and Savage were on the dance floor, dancing to classic R&B.

Britt and Savage made their way back to the VIP section as they maneuvered through the packed crowd and dancing lights. Big D's fat ass was pouring a bottle of Ace of Spades down one of the groupies' mouth as everybody laughed and enjoyed the scene.

Paying the hood rats no mind Britt, cuddled in the corner with Savage, listening to the R&B blaring through the club.

"Babe, you know I want to spend the rest of my life with you," Savage told Britt as he lifted her chin and stared in her green eyes.

"Shit, nigga, you better," she said jokingly, as she kissed his soft lips.

"Good. So I want to know if you, Ms. Brittany Jones, will marry me," Savage asked loudly, getting on one knee and opening a wedding ring box.

"Dammmmn," one of the groupies shouted, wishing it was her.

"Oh my god, Randall. Yes, yes, yes, baby, I'll marry you. I love you so much," she screamed with tears as he put the biggest diamond she'd ever seen on her finger.

"I guess I'm the best man," Big D stated in a drunken slur.

"Of course, I wouldn't have it no other way, big man. We family," Savage said, giving him a firm handshake.

When the party was over for them, they all made their way outside to depart. Big D had two groupies with him. They were strippers, who were ready to have a good time.

Britt and Savage were both on cloud nine. They felt as if they were the new Bonnie and Clyde of Miami.

***

"Yo, Bootz, that's them niggas right there," one of Bootz shooters yelled from the backseat with excitement.

The look in Bootz eyes said it all. He couldn't figure out how Big D could afford a new Bugatti, better yet, fit in one. He'd been hustling eight years and he couldn't even afford a BMW. His credit was so bad that he had to lease it in his girl's name, who also had bad credit.

"I got a plan. We can't let them get away, so you three hop out and empty y'all clip," Bootz said. They followed his orders and exited the car, ducking and walking towards their victims.

***

"You Savage, bruh. Thanks for everything, folk, you too, Britt. I love y'all more than anything," Big D said, stumbling into the parking lot area with Ariel and Gina on his muscular arms. Before Britt or Savage could respond, Britt saw a fast shadow creep from the corner of her eyes.

"It's a set up," Britt yelled as she pulled out a .357 from her purse and started busting wild shots at the three masked men, who were running and ducking behind cars as they shot back.

"Britt, get down," Savage said as he shot one of the gunmen in the head who had the drop on her.

Bloc. Bloc. Bloc. Bloc. Britt emptied her last bullets into the neck of the second gunman.

"Stay here," Savage told Britt as she sat on the ground, looking for the last gunman. Savage ran through cars to help Big D, who was near Ariel and Gina's dead bodies.

Big D snuck up behind the last gunman, who looked scared as hell while he ducked behind a Ford Explorer.

"Try again, pussy nigga." Boom, Boom, Boom. Big D split his skull in half as blood poured onto the ground like a leaky sink.

Sirens could be heard, making them jump to attention. Not wanting to get into it with the police, they had to go.

"Meet us at the condo," Savage told Big D as he helped Britt into the Bentley. Big D made it to his Bugatti, unaware of the shadow lurking in the dark. As soon as Savage pulled off, Big D dug in his pockets for his keys, but he came up short as he felt cold steel pressed against the back of his head.

"Turn around," Bootz said as he backed up with an AK-47 in his hand. Big D spit clean in his face, making Bootz laugh.

Tat, tat, tat, tat, tat, tat, tat, tat. Bootz left his lifeless body slumped on the hood of his Bugatti with his cerebellum and his medulla oblongata splattered all over the Bugatti's windshield.

Savage and Britt heard the shots. They looked in the rearview mirror to see Big D slumped on his car as a gunman they'd never seen ran into the darkness.

"Fuck," Savage yelled as Britt let off shots out her window towards the gunman in the parking lot.

"Chill, it's over," Savage said, making a right turn as the police raced down the opposite side of the street. The ride home was quiet, but the two heard each other tears for the loss of their best friend.

Chapter 35

Trust No Bitch
Weeks Later

Big D's funeral took place two weeks later in North Miami. Hundreds attended, with the exception of his mom, who was too busy looking for her next hit on the glass dick.

The crew sat in the front in pain for the loss of a person who was loyal, and had been close to them since day one. It was a sad day for the crew, but karma was near.

***

Hours later, Savage held a get together in the warehouse located in South Miami, near Court Street, where his crew had taken over. Savage gave orders for his team to raise the murder rate and kill every MPM member, but still focus on getting money.

"I put word out to the streets, and a bag on Bootz head, and niggas already spilling the beans, bro. how about I was fucking this little bitch named Rihanna from Overtown and she was Bootz side bitch. She said the nigga was bragging how he killed Big D," Bama said as Savage shook his head.

"Send the shooter after you get his whereabouts," Savage replied.

"That's already done. I'll hit you when it's done, can't leave no loose ends," Bama said as he walked out, leaving Savage with six bodyguards, all strapped up and ready to kill for their boss.

***

Overtown, Miami

Later that night, Bama parked outside Rihanna's crib, laying on his vic for the night, with assassins. Bama saw an all red Benz with dark tint pull up in front of Rihanna's small apartment complex.

Bootz hopped out, wearing a black and red dickie outfit, while Rihanna wore a white, one piece, Balmain dress, which hugged her curves and breasts. She was sexy and light skinned, with a pretty face, hazel almond eyes, and thick physique. She was a big ole freak. She could swallow a Sprite bottle.

He ran upstairs in her apartment, ready to fuck. She was just as horny. Her daughter was with her mom for the weekend, so she was litty. Bootz ran to take a piss in her bathroom, while she got naked, leaving on only her Jimmy Choo pumps.

"Damn, shawty, you waste no time," Bootz said as he walked towards her naked body, undressing.

"I love sucking your dick," she said sexually, as she grabbed his dick out of his Polo boxers, and started kissing and licking it like a porn star. Bootz was so caught up in the blow job, he didn't see four masked men creep into the room. Once Rihanna stopped bopping her head on his dick, he got angry and opened his eyes.

"Bitch, who told you to," was all he could say before he pissed himself as pre-cum leaked down his leg.

"I should of nutted in your mouth, bitch," Bootz yelled to Rihanna, who had a smile on her face as cum stained the corners of her mouth.

"That's fucked up, bruh," Fresh said, taking off his mask as everyone followed. Bootz became angry at the sight of Fresh.

"Fuck you, Fresh, and your dead brother," Bootz yelled, trying to play tough. Fresh wasted no time in pistol whipping Bootz until he passed out and woke up again.

"Now you back, where can I find Killer?" Bama asked him, standing over him with his pistol in his face.

Bootz had teeth and blood all over the floor, and his jaw was broken.

"Killer at your mama house, fucking her," he said with a chuckle, spitting out blood. Lil Shooter thought the comment was also funny, as he laughed.

"Okay, funny guy," Bama said as he put four bullets from his Glock 40 in his head. He looked at his crew and they did the same.

Rihanna was in the corner holding her ears, crying, hoping her neighbors didn't hear the loud gunshots. But she knew they did.

"I thought you said you was only going to beat him up, then rob him. You killed him in my house," Rihanna cried out as tears flooded her face.

"I know. I'm sorry. Just promise you won't tell nobody what you saw," Bama said, holding her frail shoulder.

"I don't know. It's a fucking dead man on my floor," she said in a panicked voice.

"We gotta go, folk," Lil Shooter said, looking out her bedroom window and reminding him that killing wasn't legal.

"Okay. I'ma miss you, RiRi," Bama said before he put two hollow tip bullets in her forehead.

"You can never trust a bitch," Fresh said, laughing.

"I feel you, bruh, but fuck all that. Let's go to Checkers or McDonalds, I'm fucking starving," Bama said as he turned around and spit on Bootz lifeless body for good measures.

Luckily, by the time they made it outside, there were no police in the quiet neighborhood.

Chapter 36

No Rules

Days Later

Savage received an emergency text message from Jada, saying she needed to speak to him. Savage was now parked in front of Jada's rundown building, wondering what she could want because he had too much going on already.

Moments later, Jada came out of her lobby, wearing a pair of red boy shorts with her pussy print poking out and ass hanging out.

"Hey, sorry to hear about Big D," she said as soon as she hopped in his Lexus. Savage nodded his head, trying not to look at her hard nipples poking out of her wife beater.

"What's the emergency?" he asked, cutting no corners.

"Oh yeah, yesterday, I was at my home girl house, named Tiff. I went to use her bathroom, and her boyfriend was in there, and I over heard him say he was putting a half of mill on your head," Jada said sadly.

"Who is he?" Savage said with a chuckle.

"It's not funny. He wants you dead, and you laughing? His name is Killer," she said as he looked her in her eyes seriously.

"Where can I find him?" he asked her. She was in tears, wondering if he was going die, because she loved him. Jada was in deep thought because she knew someone was about to die. And she would never forgive herself if she let anything happen to Savage.

She wrote down Tiff's address and took a deep breath.

"You lucky I love you. And good luck on your marriage," she said sadly as she kissed him on his lips before exiting his car. Savage was caught off guard. He watched her ass jiggle and her hips sway with every motion. Then he felt his dick harden. Savage pulled off and turned up the Young Jeezy album with one thing on his mind, and that was the piece of paper in his hand.

***

Tiff had been vomiting, lazy, and sick for the past couple of days, so she went to the clinic for a checkup, thinking she'd caught a virus, but she was pregnant.

She hadn't found the right time to tell Killer because his life had been crazy lately. She didn't want to stress him. She watched TV, waiting for him to come home. Lately, that was her life, always waiting on him to come home.

***

Porky Projects

"Dime, I feel like it's my fault the homie six feet," Killer told his childhood friend, Dime, who'd just come home from the feds in PA. The goons were out and lurking in the Porky PJs, the most dangerous hood in Miami. But the MPM crew ran the hood.

"We going to get them clowns, just be cool," Dime said in his smooth voice as he sipped out of the Henny bottle.

"Tight, I'm ok," Killer said as he hopped in his Camaro, heading home to spend time with Tiff and get some sleep. As soon as he came through the door stumbling into the crib, Tiff went off.

"Killer, where the fuck you been? You on some weak ass, fuck boy shit," she yelled in his face, as he walked towards the kitchen.

"Nigga, that's why I'm pregnant," she yelled. He stopped dead in his tracks and did a 360.

"Bitch, you pregnant by who? You trying to trap me but that shit ain't mines," he yelled in her face as he walked out, leaving her crying like a baby, wishing she wasn't pregnant by him, but she was.

***

"Damn, babe, you hit my g-spot every time. I gotta get used to this. And next time, I'ma swallow all that nut. It taste too good to waste," Britt said with an evil grin. The two had been fucking for two hours, like two horny dogs in heat.

"Okay, I'ma hold you to that. I'ma go shower up," Savage said, getting out the Versace sheets naked as she admired his sexy chiseled muscular body.

"Baby, I'ma get a wedding planner and a designer this week," Britt yelled as she wiped down two Desert Eagle pistols that were in Savage's holsters.

"Okay, and make sure you contact everybody on both ends of our families," he yelled from the shower.

"Yeah, that includes your mom, who you need to go see," she said, now face to face with him as she climbed into the shower and bent over in front of him. Water soaked her body while Savage fucked her slowly from behind until they both came.

Chapter 37

War Ready

Bama, Fresh, and Lil Shooter had been sitting patiently in a black Dodge minivan outside of Tiff's crib, waiting on Killer, for hours. Fresh and Lil Shooter were going back and forth about the bitch they ran a train on the previous night, and who she said had the better pipe game.

"Nigga, shut the fuck up. Look, them headlights," Bama said getting irritated with his crew's idle talk.

Tiff climbed out of an all-white Porsche Cayman, but she was alone, with a couple of shopping bags. That pissed Bama off even more than he already was.

"I'm sick of playing hide and sneak. We should make her call his bitch ass," Bama stated as he watched the beautiful woman walk into the nice two story house.

"Let's send him a message, but this neighborhood looks to quiet, bruh. They got a neighborhood watch signs, my nigga," Lil Shooter said.

"Fuck that. Come on," Bama said as he hopped out.

***

Tiff was about to take a shower and go to sleep. She'd had a long day at the doctor's office, and shopping for her future baby. Killer hadn't been home in two days, and she didn't care. She was having a baby, with him, or without. Tiff was in her kitchen, preparing a quick snack. She was so deep into her yogurt, she didn't even notice the three men with dreads in front of her.

"Damn, nice kitchen," Fresh said, looking around at the stainless steel kitchen.

"Oh my god," she screamed, dropping her snack on the floor. "What do you want? Killer's not here, and it's no money here," she stated, knowing the game.

"Sorry, this ain't no robbery, or a rape. We don't want your washed up pussy. We want Killer, bitch," Fresh demanded.

"Well you see he not here, so get the fuck out, before I call police," she shouted as if she was in control, until Bama slapped her so hard with his pistol that it echoed through the whole house.

She fell off the stool, holding her stomach, trying to get herself together.

"I'ma ask your dumb ass one more 'gain, where is he?" Bama asked with fire in his eyes as he placed his gun in her mouth.

"He's normally in Porky or MLK," Tiff said, crying.

"Thank you," he said as he placed the gun to her head.

"Hold on, please. I told you everything. I'm pregnant," she shouted as he laughed and blew her brains out.

***

Killer was in a nearby strip club, drinking Cîroc out of the bottle, throwing money on the naked dancer. Tiff added stress to his stressful life. It was not the right time to bring a child into his crazy life.

Asia's number popped up on his caller ID. He was hoping she was ready to give up some pussy. She was Tiff's best friend, and a model. As soon as he answered, Asia was yelling, so he couldn't clearly make out what she was saying. All he heard was Tiff was shot and she was in the hospital. Killer ran out of the club and sped to the hospital with his goons.

Ten minutes later, the hospital was crowded with Tiff's friends, family, and other civilians.

"I'ma have you put in jail, you fucking murderer," Sophia yelled. She tried to attack Killer because she though he was the reason why the doctor told her that her niece wouldn't make it.

"Asia, what's going on?" he asked Asia as she was wiping her puffy, colorful eyes.

"She dead, Killer. She was DOA," she said. Killer sat down, not realizing tears were falling from his eyes.

Chapter 38

Confessions
Weeks Later

"Gentlemen, prepare yourself for this big mission. We have two main suspects that are wanted for the murder of Anthony Wilson, aka Bootz, and over nine attempted murders in our city," Agent Joseph said, standing in the conference room, pointing at a large monitor on the wall.

"We also have some new details on the murder of a kingpin's girlfriend a couple weeks ago. A nosey neighbor said they saw our guy, Bama, and Fresh exit the victim's home," the agent said proudly.

"Let's not take this case lightly. We're dealing with heartless killers that we believe are connected to some heavy hitters," the bureau supervisor stated from the back of the room.

Agent Joseph smiled to his boss, as he looked at his ex-partner Agent Martinez, cheering him on, in the front row.

"We're also almost to a closing with the investigation of the MPM organization. I plan to kill two birds with one stone," Agent Joseph stated before he ended the meeting.

Joseph and Martinez were the worst type of agents you would want to come across. The two extorted drug dealers and sold the drugs they would steal to the hustlers they robbed. The two would raid traps and take everything. But the previous year, they'd raided a crew of Cubans and ended up killing two of them. Agent Martinez took the rap and was suspended for six months and re-assigned to a new position at a desk, at the Bureau headquarters. Meanwhile, Agent Joseph had recently made lieutenant of the FBI, and he had big plans for Miami this year.

***

Savage walked into his mom's house to the smell of soul food cooking, which was his favorite, but his mom rarely cooked nowadays, so he knew she was in good mood.

"Mom, where you at?" he said, turning down the loud TV that was playing in the living room.

"Kitchen, baby," Lisa yelled, happy her son was there. She was talking to Rich, who had pictures in his hand. Savage made small talk with the two, but he felt something was different about Rich, as if he was depressed.

"These are my children. Well they were. They will always be a part of me," Rich said, handing Savage two pictures, as Lisa rubbed his hand for comfort.

"We were at Six Flags that day. That's Lil Boo to your right, Tiff and Pole on your left," Rich said, smiling and reminiscing.

Savage looked closer and couldn't believe he was holding a picture of all three of his victims. His stomach flipped as guilt hit him.

"The streets took them. I can see no wrong in my angels," Rich said as he stood to leave. After Lisa came back from walking him out, she took a deep breath.

"I feel so sad for him," she said, as she finished baking the curry chicken in the oven.

"Mom, I got a question about my dad," Savage said, changing the subject, as chills went down her spinal cord.

"Baby, you know I don't like talking about that stuff, but shoot," Lisa replied.

"Okay, who was that close friend you mentioned that daddy had that you never trusted?" he asked as her face saddened.

"His name was Sam. he was sneaky, and just so happened, the night your father passed, Sam was on his way to meet him. The police told me that Sam and my ex-friend were the last two people in his call log. They were both questioned about his murder, but they had nothing on either one of them," she said, stirring a pot of fish stew.

"Damn, so it could've been anybody," he said.

"Yeah, Tone was no civilian. He had enemies, but sometimes your enemies are the closest ones to you, and just so happened, Sam disappeared," she said, shaking her head.

"I feel you," Savage said in deep thought. Something wasn't right.

"How's Britt? I love that girl. She's perfect for you," Lisa said with a chuckle.

"She good, mom. I gotta go get up with her now," he said, checking his Rolex bustdown watch he'd copped two days ago.

"Before you leave, sit down, I have something I've been waiting to tell you," she said, getting his full attention. "I'm pregnant," she said with a kiddy smile, as Savage almost choked on a piece of chicken. He knew she had a different glow to her, but he thought she was out in the sun more.

"Wow, that's good. Guess you never too old," he stated.

"What? Boy, please, I been had my grove back. Mommy got that snap back water. I used to have niggers going crazy," Lisa said with a laugh. He covered his ears, happy for a brother or sister on its way. The two talked and ate until it got dark out. Then he went back home.

Chapter 39

All Eyes on Me

Britt and JoJo were in the living room of her new mansion, which was worth 2.5 million. The two had been hanging out all morning, talking about college, love, and their future plans. They had a great sister and brother relationship.

JoJo liked Savage a lot, but he knew he lived a dangerous lifestyle that could land him dead or in jail, and he wanted his sister to have a bright future. He was happy for their marriage coming up, he was just happy to see her joyful.

She never told JoJo she was a part of the crew, but she knew something had to be kept undercovers. Britt told Savage to call a meeting just to make sure money was right, crews were being paid, and turfs were in order. Savage had a meeting with the connect about a new shipment in an hour or so, but everything was going smoothly.

The two chilled for a couple of hours until JoJo had to go out of town to handle some business affairs.

***

Carol City

Fresh had just left Monica's crib. She was a classy, hood rat, who looked like Jhene Aiko, but thicker, with a good state job, working at a federal prison. She was charging niggas at Coleman USP five thousand dollars for a hand job. The inmates loved her. She was one of the baddest bitches on the compound.

Fresh had just copped a new, grey Jaguar, worth over two hundred thousand dollars, straight off the lot, thanks to Monica's good credit. He was walking to his car when he felt his phone vibrate. It was a message from Britt, informing him about the big meeting tomorrow. He texted back "ok" while he hopped in the Jag, feeling a little paranoid, as he'd been lately, for some odd reason.

Fresh looked at his Draco sitting in the passenger's seat and smiled as he pulled off, not noticing two blue vans tailing him.

***

Savage had just left his connect with new weight on his shoulders because OG told him the feds were on to his crew. Savage sent all his lieutenants a "red dot" message, which meant to shut it down and lay low until they heard from him or Britt.

OG explained to him that he'd had a couple of agents on his payroll for years. That was how he knew Savage and his crew were clean, because Miami had lot of rats and snakes. He'd just copped two hundred bricks, and OG gave him fifty good measures. But he warned him to tighten up his circle because the feds were bad for business, and OG didn't need heat on him.

***

Liberty City

Jada was walking around in the treacherous part of Liberty City, wearing a tight skirt, heels, and a dirty tank top. She was on a mission to find crack. Lately, Jada's life had been flipped upside down. She'd become a straight fiend overnight, due to stress and the loss of her mom.

Lil Shooter was posted up, with his goons, on the block, enjoying the nice summer day as the trap boomed with sells.

"Turn that shit up, shawty. Blood Raw talk that struggle, bruh, besides Lil Kodak," Lil Shooter started.

"Nah, bruh, Rick Ross that nigga," a young nigga shouted, posted on top of an old hooked up Cutlass, sitting on twenty eights.

Lil Shooter was listening to his soldiers go back and forth, but when he saw a thick, sexy, dark skinned bitch walking his way,, his dick got hard as he stood beside his Benz.

"What the fuck? Jada," Lil Shooter yelled her name, once he saw her face. He was wondering why she was on this side of town, and going into his trap. Seconds later, she was rushing out and back up the block.

"Lil Rugor, you know that bitch?" he said, pointing at Jada before she hit the corner.

"Yeah, she good, boss. She been copping heavy, and niggas ran a train on her last night. Her shit fire. She sucked the life outta my dick. I never had a bitch deep throat me like that," Lil Rugor boasted.

"Look, don't serve her shit. When you see her, call me, bruh. She peoples, okay," Lil Shooter said firmly. "Nobody touch her, or that's they ass," he said, as climbed into his Benz and pulled off.

***

Britt had her legs in the air, spread open like a baldhead eagle as Savage slid his tongue and index finger in and out of her love box, which was soaked with creamy cum, as she'd nutted twice already.

Savage put his hard dick in her and went to work, making her go crazy.

"Oh shit, yessss. Baby, fuck me. Go deeper, ummmhhh," she moaned as they both nutted. Once he came in her, he grabbed a new jar of Vaseline and flipped her on her flat stomach. He placed Vaseline around her asshole and on his dick. She was ready.

Savage knew she was a virgin back there, so he took his time. He put his tip in and out, making her squirm as he got half way in. Once she got the feel, she was throwing her phat ass back on his dick, trying to take all of it up her ass.

"Ugghh. Yes, fuck my ass, daddy," she screamed.

He was sweating hard as he was putting in work. He felt himself about to bust, but he pulled out. Britt turned around so she could catch his nut, and she did just that. She swallowed every drop with a big smile, while rubbing his dick on her pretty face.

Chapter 40

Rock Bottom
Next Day

Savage called Lil Shooter bright and early, after receiving a couple of texts from him.

"What's good, homie? I was tied up last night. Sorry, but what's the 911?" Savage asked Lil Shooter.

"It's good in the hood, but guess who I saw coming out the trap," Lil Shooter said, trying to play the guessing game.

"Nigga, it's too early for this game. Just tell me. Who?"

"Okay. Jada, bruh, shawty was on it hard. And she out here fucking for a hit," Lil Shooter said, disgusted because he'd had a crush on her, a while back. He'd wanted to fuck her, but now she was a crackhead to him.

"Damn, I'ma call you later. Make sure she can't get shit from nobody," Savage said, before hanging up. He was hurt because Jada had been his friend since the sandbox. They'd even had sleepovers as kids.

Britt came out of the bathroom in a Pink towel, with her hair wrapped, singing a Keisha Cole song.

"You okay, babe?" she said when she saw a look of disappointment on his face.

"Yeah. Jada using crack, the shit I supply. I feel for her, you know. She good people," he said.

Britt laughed to herself because she couldn't care less. She knew how close the two were, but Jada had tried to cut her throat for years, and take Savage, so she really hated her.

"She will be okay. Just make a Dua for her," she said, referring to a Muslim prayer.

"I am. I wish I could help," he said, about to piss her off.

"The wedding is in a couple of days. Let's focus on the task at hand," she said, sitting in his lap on their bed, rubbing his dick.

"I'ma pick up my tuxedo today," he said, standing up to go bathe real quick, and leaving her with a sour look. She knew what was really on his mind, that crackhead bitch.

***

Later

Jada was walking out of her crib in the same clothes she'd had on for two days. She only came home to shower, then she was back on the streets. Her mother had died two weeks prior from AIDs. She was all Jada had ever had, so it crushed her. She took her first hit of rock, and never came back. She felt as if crack was her lifesaver.

Ever since she was a child, Jada's life had been fucked up. She was raped daily by her stepfather, Erik, and her mother never believed her because she was dick struck. The only person she told about being raped was Savage. This went on from the time she was ten, until she was fifteen.

One night, Erik raped her while her mom was at work. She was fourteen. Erik took a smoke break outside, preparing for round two. On the last puff of his cigarette, he felt a gun to his head.

"Look, man, take the money. Let me live, please. You can even have some young fresh pussy upstairs, just me walk away," Erik cried out.

"I'll make sure you never rape a little girl again," Savage said in his soft voice, as he blew Erik's brains onto the brick wall of Jada's building.

A day later, Jada saw Savage and cried in his arms at school. She'd seen him run away from the scene. She knew his walk, run, or voice from anywhere.

Jada kept that as their little secret, but that made their bond official. Jada walked through the dark streets, like a zombie from the Walking Dead.

An all-black Range Rover, with big black rims and dark tint, pulled up on her, stopping her. She knew whoever was in the truck had big money, so she fixed her hair and licked her chapped lips.

Once the windows rolled half way down, she wasted no time in shooting her game like a sales woman.

"Hey, daddy, let me show you a good time and what these thick lips can do," Jada said, still unaware of who was in the truck. Once the tinted windows rolled all the way down, Jada almost jumped out of her skin. She was embarrassed to see Savage.

"I'm so sorry. I ain't know it was you," she said, fumbling over her words.

"Get the fuck in the car," was all he said as she got in and went for a ride. Savage broke the silence.

"Jada, I know your mom's dead. I was at the funeral, and I paid for it. She was family," Savage said, as Jada put her head down. She'd wondered who paid for her mom's funeral because she had no wills and no type of life support systems.

"Thanks," she said.

"I also know you getting high. What the fuck is wrong with you, Jada? This ain't you," he yelled as he stopped at a red light.

She started crying. "My life is over. I have nothing. You don't know how I feel. I'm blessed not to have HIV, but I'm still dying slowly," she replied.

"Look, I'ma always be here, but you not using drugs no more, or selling your body. You're too beautiful and special," he said, wiping way her tears.

"I know," she mumbled.

"I'm taking you to a rehab center, so you can get your life back. And when you get out, I will have a job, crib and car for you. Take this, also, and if I ever hear you did a drug again, I'ma kill you and them," he said seriously. Then he gave her an envelope full of money, as he parked in front of a rehab center.

Jada wanted to hop out of the car and run with the money, but she knew Savage would find her in minutes. His crew ran the city.

"Okay, I'ma do it, but don't forget about me," she said, as she hopped out and walked into the clinic.

"Hey, I'm Jada Barnes, and I'm here to start my recovery," she told the clerk at the desk, who was smiling at her, proud of her strength as a young woman to get help.

"Good, you're right on time, Ms. Barnes. We've been waiting on you. Everything is ready and fully paid for on your behalf," the older woman said. She was a recovering addict herself. Jada saw Savage pull off, and smiled. She knew he really had genuine love for her.

***

Downtown Miami

Britt was wedding dress shopping with her friend, Kim, who was her bridesmaid.

"Girl, I hope Savage got some sexy friends, other than Bama. I hate his crazy ass."

"Damn, hoe, don't you fuck with Tails, that kid from Brooklyn, who runs some projects?" Lisa said, trying on a Harve Leger dress in the dressing room.

"Girl, that's my boo. He got locked up for some murders he did in New York. I know he's facing life, so I gotta move on. Fuck all that, his loss. But did you hear about Jada, uhmmm," Kim said.

"Yeah, but I don't care, to be honest," Britt said, looking at her curves, smiling.

"Them O-Town niggas videotaped her sucking dick and getting gangbanged. They run with your hubby," she said.

"So, fuck her. How this dress look?" Britt asked, spinning around as the designer and Kim nodded their heads.

"Good, I'll take it, and I'll pay the 150k in cash," she said, grabbing her Dolce & Gabbana bag. Britt loved her wedding dress. Now she had to go meet the wedding planner.

Chapter 41
Fed Band

Killer had just left Tiff's gravesite. It was a hot summer day, so snakes flooded the high, uncut grass. He was drinking Henny in the 90 degree weather, trying to ease his pain. When she was buried, he was home, in his low key condo near South Beach Blvd. He just couldn't see the love of his life put six feet into the ground. The feds had just snatched thirty-five of his most loyal soldiers the previous night, for murders, drugs, and home invasions. He knew he was number one on the indictment list, but he wasn't going down easily. He'd lost everything within months, thanks to Savage's crew. Killer had some leftover business he needed to attend to. Then he had plans to chill with his Mexican connect until shit died down in the 305.

***

FBI

"Ladies and Gentlemen, we now have two accurate locations on our targets," Agent Joseph stated, standing in front of his raid team. They were all geared up, ready for war.

"Don't fuck this up, or I will make sure you will answer calls at the front desk, with Martinez, until you retire," Agent Joseph yelled.

The agents all gathered in four different vans, in front of Wal-Mart, at midnight. Two vans were going in two different directions.

***

Liberty City

Fresh was just leaving one of his trap houses, checking on his workers. He was clean in his Balmain jeans and shirt. He was in his sky blue ALK Benz, on his way to a meeting to holla at the crew.

He also wanted to swing by DeDe's crib in Cord City for some quick head. She could make any nigga cum in ten seconds.

With business on his mind, he knew some head could wait. As he drove down Main St, he noticed two black vans creeping up behind him, from side blocks. Fresh thought nothing of it, until the vans were on his bumper and the sirens came on.

"Fuck, bruh," he yelled, hitting the wood grain steering wheel. Fresh hit the gas, running lights and stop signs, like a mad man, and almost causing two accidents. He was doing ninety-five miles per hours. He grabbed the Draco from the passenger's seat and put it in his lap. Then he remembered he had an AK-47 and six bricks in his trunk,

He took the feds on a wild chase. They couldn't keep up with the Benz coupe as it swerved through traffic.

"What the fuck?" the agents said, as bullets almost shattered the windows. Fresh tried to shoot out their windows with the Draco, but he ended up hitting one of the agents in the next van, making the driver crash into a light pole.

"Man down, van down, man down, send the backup team to North Blvd and 5th Ave. we're in a high speed chase with our target," Agent Joseph yelled into his walkie-talkie.

Fresh felt like he was in a movie, as a Future album played in the background. As bullets took out his back windows, the agents were on his tail.

He pushed 115 mph downhill as he saw train tracks near. He knew a train would be coming within seconds, as the red lights flashed at the crossing.

"What the fuck does he think he's doing? We can't make that shit boss," the driver said nervously.

"Just fucking drive. Miami PD is behind us. He's trying to fake us out," Agent Joseph shouted, dodging Bullets from Fresh, as he sent shots back from his own weapon. He was getting pissed off because the hoodlum was still alive.

Fresh did 121 mph, breaking the warning barrier, but the train smacked the midsection and back end of the Benz, causing it to flip and killing Fresh with the powerful impact. His body flew out the windshield. There was also a white powdery substance that flew everywhere. Agent Joseph was smiling at the sight of Fresh's dead body, folded like a pretzel. Once the other agents, and Miami's forensic team, arrived, they took over. The agent that Fresh shot was pronounced dead at the scene of the accident from a wound to the neck.

***

Bama had just stepped out of his crib, ready to make his way to the meeting across town. It was 12:30am. The streets were quiet, and Bama wanted to ride his bike, instead of taking his Benz.

When he made it to the driveway, he saw a beautiful white chick, who looked like Kylie Jenner. She wore tights and running shoes, as she jogged past. The two waved, while Bama admired her nice, round ass jiggling.

He checked his hip for his gun, but he felt nothing. He must have left it inside while he rushed out, not wanting wake Big Curt. As soon as he turned around, agents appeared from everywhere with assault rifles and big lights.

"Get the fuck down, now, fucker, before I blow your brains out," an agent yelled. Bama had his hands in the air, getting down on the grass, surrendering.

Two hours later, across town in a low key federal building few knew about, Bama sat in a cold, dim interrogation room, cuffed to a steel table, with mirrors everywhere.

Agents stood on the other side of the mirrors, watching his every move for over an hour.

"It's time. Come on," Agent Joseph said as he walked into the room with two more agents and the pretty white woman that had been jogging near Bama's house.

As soon as they walked in, Bama laughed out loud and shook his head at the blue-eyed devils.

"I'm glad you have a good sense of humor. Let's see if you laugh about your murder charge, you fucking faggot. You're being charged with the murder of Bootz, and we have enough attempted murders to get you the chair, asshole," Agent Joseph yelled in his face, as Bama sat there silently.

"I'ma make you a one-time deal. Help me help you because you're only a little fish, but I want Savage. If you help us set your friend up, you're a free man, no murder charge. You may have to do 5-10 years for the discharge of a weapon, according to Section 924 Co, but we can make up some fake paperwork so you won't get stabbed to death in a penitentiary," Agent Joseph said proudly.

"Okay, I'ma give you someone bigger than me, or anyone you know. This will be your big break, and I know you thirsty for him," Bama said, finally speaking.

The agents were all happy, except the white chick. She had heard so much about Savage's crew, and for him to break so easily, she was disgusted. She hated rats.

"Tell us, man. We going to take of you," Agent Joseph stated with excitement.

"Okay, his name is D's nuts," Bama said, laughing so hard he almost fell out the chair. Even the sexy female agent chuckled a couple of times because he had had Agent Joseph going.

"I'ma make sure somebody fucks you in the ass when you go to Big Sandy or Pollock, or somewhere," Agent Joseph yelled.

"Yeah, and I'ma fuck your daughter in her ass with this big black dick, and give you mixed grandbabies," Bama yelled, making the white girl blush at the thought of the size of his dick.

The agents left the room. When he asked for a phone call, he was denied many times. But his lawyer, Mr. Lawrence, was already on his way and paid in full, thanks to Savage.

Thirty minutes later, the white female agent walked in alone with a notepad and pen. She wore her long, blond hair in a ponytail, and Gucci glasses, showing her beautiful features.

"Your friend, Fresh, was killed in a police chase. He also killed an agent. So you got a lot on your back. Take my personal number, I can help you someday," she said, licking her lips as she stood to leave. Nobody was behind the mirrors or recording, so she made her move.

Bama sat there for hours thinking about Fresh. He knew he wasn't going out easily, but he still felt pain for his friend.

Chapter 42

Bad News

Savage woke up and called the lawyer to find out what was what with Bama. He'd already seen Fresh's death on the news. Mr. Lawrence told him that Bama would be held with no bond until he could see the magistrate judge, in three days.

Britt canceled the meeting at the last minute, when Big Curt called her and told her what happened to his son, and how the feds raided the crib.

Fresh and Bama were all over the news. While Britt was sleep, Savage watched it every hour. But the main shit that sparked the media attention was the death of an agent.

Savage went to make Salat, his afternoon prayer, hoping Allah would protect his friends and family. Mr. Lawrence had been on his payroll for a while. He was an Ivy League graduate, and the best black lawyer in the Florida Associate Bar Academy, so he had a lot of pull in the jurisdiction.

***

Dade County

Killer was flipping through the TV channels in his new side bitch's crib. He'd met her in the strip club months ago. He only recently wifed her so he could hide out in her crib until he was ready to move forward with his plan.

Killer saw Fresh and Bama's faces on the news channel, which made him stop and listen. He smiled to himself because now his plan would be simpler.

He'd spoken to his connect, Montanta, the previous day, and he was waiting on his friend. Montanta was the leader of a very powerful cartel family, bigger than El Chapo's family. Killer and Montanta had been best friends ever since they met, years ago, in Mexico City. Killer sat on the couch as Shontell came out of the back room, naked. She was a black, young dancer, with a nice body. She got on her knees and took his dick in her mouth. She went to work, while playing in her pussy.

***

Days Later

Bama made it to Miami federal holdover, where he could start his bid. Once he entered the building, he was being treated like Big Meech.

He was in his cell, unpacking, when a pretty, female CO informed him that he had a legal visit. He did some pushups, brushed he teeth, and fixed his clothes. Then he made his way downstairs.

Once he made it into the visiting room, he was placed in a small booth with a glass and a phone. Mr. Lawrence walked in wearing an Armani suit, looking like money.

"Good morning, Mr. Smith," the lawyer said.

Bama just nodded his head as he picked up the phone, hoping this black nigga was the new Johnnie Cochran.

"I'm sure you know they got you for murder. Do you have worries or questions?" he asked calmly.

"I do, black man. Are you a sellout, or a fighter for equality and justice, for the people?" Bama asked sternly, as the lawyer took off his Prada glasses.

"Listen, I've never been a sellout to the blacks. My willpower and struggle won't let me," he stated sternly, staring into Bama's eyes, letting him know it was real business on his behalf.

"Now I got questions. Have you made any 5KL agreements? Any proffer agreements? Have you said anything that is discriminating to us if we got to trial?" he asked.

"I will never. My honor is all I have," Bama said.

"Good. I already know. I did my research. You can hold water, unlike a lot of niggers these days," Mr. Lawrence said honestly. "Now let's work. I'ma be real, there is an offer for 80-100 years on the table now, and your bail was denied, due to the high profile case."

"If I blow trial, how long?" he asked sadly.

"If you blow trail, you can get a couple of life sentences, to be honest. But the chance of an appeal is 98%. It's on you," he replied.

"Let's go to trial. File the motions this week," Bama stated as he stood up to leave.

Chapter 43

Big Art
North Miami

Savage was at his Friday Jummah service in the packed mosque. He still prayed, fasted, and went to Jummah, because Islam was his religion, and in his heart.

The Muslims in Miami were from all different backgrounds, races, and ethnicities. Savage had recently bought the lease for the mosque, since they were going through financial issues.

There was a new brother in the mosque, Adbulla Haffeeza (servants for protector), aka Big Art. He was a real live killer and robber. He'd just came home from a fourteen year fed bid. He was huge at 6'5" and 285 pounds of muscles, with long dreads. At the age of 36, he was now mature and focused.

"Salaam – Alaikum," Savage greeted Big Art.

"Wa'alaikum Salaam," Big Art replied as he looked at the young brother who came to the mosque every Friday. Big Art watched Savage closely, and he could tell he was somebody. Plus, his name in the streets was like Larry Hoover.

"You just came home, ahkee?" Savage asked, as the mosque started to clear out because Jummah was done.

"I just did fourteen years in the USP maximum security prisons. I'm just trying to get my life together now, and stay out," Big Art said.

"I'm glad. Look, take my number. I own a couple of small businesses, and we could always use the help. Take it, please," Savage said, handing him his card with his business number on it.

"Thank you. I'll be sure to reach out," Big Art said before he left the mosque.

***

Big Art's birth name was Prince Edward. He'd grown up in Gonaives, Haiti, where he struggled day by day. His father, Taino, was a drug lord, who was murdered by his own soldiers. His mother was a devoted Protestant, who gave herself to the Lord.

At the young age of fifteen years old, he was already 6 feet and 190 pounds, all muscle. But instead of football and college, he turned to killing and robbing drug dealers.

Before he was eighteen, he had over twenty bodies under his belt. But when his mom died of cancer, he became ruthless and homeless. He met another Haitian, who lived in the states, and was able to get him a green card.

As time passed, Big Art started robbing drug dealers from New York to Texas. He made almost two million in one year off of licks.

Big Art knew he had enemies, but he had no clue the Feds would be the number one enemy as he started to get sloppy with his work, leaving DNA all over the crib and his victims cars.

His biggest mistake was when he robbed and killed a Cuban Kingpin in Tampa, Florida, leaving a witness who was hiding in the kitchen. She'd seen everything. She was a loyal maid.

Minutes later, the FBI had everything they needed to arrest Big Art. Even though they knew he'd done a lot more shit, they only had evidence for one case. They had DNA and a loyal witness. He was arrested in Cali for the murder of the Cuban drug lord.

With a good lawyer, he was able to cop out to thirty years. But a couple of new laws dropped, and he was able to cut his sentence in half. He became a Muslim in prison, thanks to his celly, a Muslim named Maine from New York. He'd been Muslim for over ten years.

Chapter 44

Lost and Found

Lil Shooter wasn't taking Fresh's death well. Lately, they'd become best friends, and he vowed to honor his friend's name by killing every MPM member.

It was Savage's wedding day and he supposed to attend but he had plans to put in some work. He rode around, strapped up, in his black Yukon truck.

Just so happened, it was four pm and he was riding past Wendy's restaurant. He saw two MPM members dressed in all red, laughing and playing.

Lil Shooter decided to spin the block. He bust a U-turn, laying on his victims.

***

"Rick, I'm telling you, blood, Club Mansion was turned up last night. The Migos came out and crushed it. We was forty deep, bruh," Fab said, getting hyped up as Rick shook his head, as if he was there.

"Damn, I was deep in some pussy," Rick replied as Lil Shooter approached both of them as if he knew them.

"Tell Killer I will see him." Boom. Boom. Boom.

Fab tried to run as Rick took his last breath. Lil Shooter put five rounds in Fab's back. Then he walked up to him and shot him twice in his temple. He ran off in a tuxedo suit and Michael Kors shoes, with blood stains on them.

***

Savage had been so busy, lately, with Fresh's death, Bama's case, finding Killer, and his wedding that he forgot he had a sit down with OG, his plug.

Once at the mansion, Savage had his goons post up outside, as always, as he went in to get searched. Then he made his way to the back yard.

Normally, there would be beautiful, half-naked women running around in bikinis. But the women were trained to kill and OG always had them around. Savage always paid close attention to small details in life.

OG was sitting on the edge of the pool, showing his chiseled body.

"Good afternoon, kid. How are you?" OG said as he put on his Versace robe.

"I'm good. Where are all the women?" he asked.

"In DR at training camp," he said as he walked over to the small table to pour himself a cup of fresh grapefruit juice.

"Drink?" OG offered.

"No, thank you," he replied.

"Sorry about Fresh. I send my condolences," OG said sadly.

"Thanks. How do you know everything when you never move?" Savage asked.

"I know everything about people I deal with," he replied, taking a sip of his juice.

"Damn, I don't even know your real name, or where you're from," Savage said with a laugh. He only knew him as OG.

"You never asked, kid. That's why it's good to ask questions. It's no such thing as a bad question. My name is Sammy, most call me Sam. I was born and raised in Brooklyn. Boy, it was rough growing up. But I met a plug, and my life changed," he said, laughing.

Savage wanted to tell him his family was from Brooklyn, but he kept going.

"I only had one good friend. You gotta value friends. But when I found out he killed my brother, I had to unfriend him," OG stated with glossy eyes.

"I was never a killer. I was hustler, big time, with a low profile, ever since I did my up north bid. The night I took Tone's life in that hospital parking lot, it killed a part of me. But I had to, karma is a part of life," OG said zoned out.

Savage's head went from 0 to 60 within seconds.

"His wife, Lisa, was beautiful. She hated me, but it's a part of life," OG said as he looked up to see an awkward look on Savage's face.

"You good, young blood?" OG asked.

Savage snapped out of it, getting his poker face together for then nigga who killed his pops.

"I'm good, just listening, OG. When is the next drop off? The money is all in position," Savage said.

"In a couple of days. You about your money, so I'ma double you up and send you a wedding gift. Congratulations," OG said, smiling and raising his glass as if to do a cheers alone.

"Damn, my bad. You're more than welcome to come."

"Nah, I gotta go out to Las Vegas to handle business. But you have a beautiful woman, take care of her," OG said, making Savage uncomfortable.

The two laughed, joked, and talked some more before they parted ways. They went different ways with different agendas on their minds.

Chapter 45

Death Wish

Lisa was cuddled up with Rich on the living couch, watching the Martin Show, laughing and enjoying themselves.

"Please, be ready in an hour. We can't be late for Randall's wedding," Lisa stated as she stood up in her tights, showing her thick curves, camel toe, and her big pudgy stomach.

"Okay, baby, I know. I wouldn't miss it for the world," Rich stated as Lisa wobbled towards the kitchen to make breakfast.

They both heard two loud knocks at the door. "I got it, babe," he yelled as he went to see who it was.

When Lisa heard nothing, she made her way to the front door.

"Who is it?" Lisa stopped dead in her tracks when she saw two guns pointed at Rich. Now there were two pointed at her. Rich already had blood leaking from his nose, as if he was pistol whipped before she came out of the kitchen.

"Jesus, please, save me," was all she could say as Rich recognize one of the gunmen.

"Killer, is that you? What is this about?" Rich said, fixing his glasses. He'd known Killer since he was a baby. He used to always have him over the house for sleepovers.

"Nigga, both of y'all sit the fuck down. I ask the damn questions," Killer said with fire in his eyes.

Lisa and Rich did as they were told, but she wondered how the two knew each other.

"I'm looking for Savage, but since I can't get him, then his mom is the next best thing," Killer said.

Rich had heard the name before, and it wasn't good.

"What does this have to do with us? I don't get it," Rich yelled at Killer, until he was on top of him, pistol whipping him.

"Now shut the fuck up," Killer said, taking a break because his wrist hurt.

Rich's face was swollen and bloody.

"Her son killed my friends and my pregnant finance, so you both gotta pay. This bitch's son killed your kids, and you fucking her," Killer said, laughing.

"No, he didn't, Rich. My baby isn't a Savage. Don't listen to him. He's the devil," she cried out loud.

Killer jumped on her like a mad man and started pistol whipping her until she was unconscious, laying in her own puddle of blood.

"John John, give Rich your gun, now," Killer said to one of his gunmen, who followed Killers orders.

"Rich, take that gun in your hand and kill that bitch. Serve justice for your kids," Killer said smoothly, as Lisa started to wake up.

As he looked at her and their unborn seed, Rich's emotions were on a rollercoaster. He pictured himself shooting her ten times in his head, but his heart couldn't do it.

"Rich, you a sucker. I heard you was a killer back in the days. I guess them days been over. Give me my damn gun back," Killer said.

Rich raised the gun at Killer, and all of Killer's men aimed their pistols at him.

Killer laughed. "Put y'all guns down. Pull the trigger, Rich," Killer said.

Rich wasted no time. He pulled it twice, getting a click sound. He realize it was unloaded.

"You think I'm dumb, nigga? Goodbye," Killer said as he filled Rich and Lisa's bodies with bullets before exiting the house. Killer hopped in the Dodge truck outside and pulled off, listening to 2pac's *Hail Mary*. He lit a blunt and headed to his next pit stop.

Chapter 46

Wedding Time

Life was stressful but that wasn't going to stop Savage from enjoying the happiest day of his life, marrying Britt. He had put everything to the side for this day, including beef, Sam, drugs, and the streets. Savage walked into his kitchen to see women all over the place in his mansion. Some were preparing food, clothes, flowers, all types of shit was going on.

Britt came out of the kitchen bathroom on the phone, shouting orders to someone on the other end. Normally, she was sweet, but today was her big day everything had to go right.

She took the conversation upstairs for privacy, and Savage followed. Once in the room, Britt rubbed his muscular shoulders, admiring his tattoos all over, and his long dreads, held in a ponytail.

"I want everything to be perfect for us today," he said.

"Don't worry about that, babe," she said, knowing there was something else he was hiding. She knew him too well.

"I need you to add a good brother named Big Art to the guest list. I've been dealing with him, lately, and I think he can be a big help to the family. Plus, with Bama and Fresh gone, we need more honorable men," Savage said as Britt nodded.

"I spoke to Mr. Lawrence. He said Bama going to trial, and he stuck to the g-code."

"Yeah, we cut from a different cloth. Snitching or folding not in us, we rather be carried by six than judged by twelve crackers. Fresh will always be remembered, and we going to fight for Bama's freedom," he said as Britt got up and made her way out of the room.

"I love you, Randall, until I'm carried by six," she said before walking out of the room.

***

Hours Later

The church was packed inside and outside, like a night club. Everybody was dressed to impress to see the King of Miami take his vows.

Lil Shooter and Big Art were in one of the back rooms, chopping it up, getting to know each other. Lil Shooter had also brought his cousin, Lil Snoop, who had a big name in Jacksonville and parts of Miami.

Savage walked into the room, looking like money in his tuxedo. Lil Shooter had on a tuxedo, also, while Big Art wore an Armani Suit. Lil Snoop walked into the room, dripping Gucci, with his young face and long hair. He was Snoop Dog's twin.

"Gentlemen, this is a new start. We're about to embark on a new level of success. But there will be a lot of deadly missions, like the one I have planned soon. You three men are the chosen. This is the new family. If anyone don't want to be a part, leave now. No hard feelings, it's only business," Savage said, looking around.

"Good. Now we took over all MPM turfs, next is the Zoe Pounds. And then we go after my connect. It's going to get real after today. In this family, we feel the same pain," Savage stated as he grabbed four bottles of Armand De Brignac champagne, which was one of the most expensive champagne brands in the world.

They all cheered and popped bottles, ready for the future. Savage stepped out the room to call his mother for the third time, only to get her voicemail.

"You good, ahkee?" Big Art asked.

"I hope so. But I got a feeling something's not right. Lil Shooter, send a crew to my mom's house, right now," Savage said, walking down the hall.

Lil Shooter made the call and his goons were on it. But the wedding would be starting in a couple of minutes, so Savage had to focus, as he made his way to the alter.

Britt walked with JoJo down the aisle, as held her hand. Everybody eyed her dress, some hated, and some were amazed at how beautiful she was.

Once the bride and groom were face to face, the Iman began the ceremony. After their vows were exchanged, it was over. Everybody yelled and screamed as people started to exit out of the front entrance.

Outside, there was a Rolls Royce limo waiting for the newlyweds. Britt tossed her flowers and, of course, her best friend, Kim, caught them, after pushing two women out the way.

At the drop of a dime, four gunmen, dressed in all black, ran down on the crowd and started firing rounds from assault rifles, high powered ones.

The crowd ran in panic mode. Savage pushed Britt to the ground, so she wouldn't get hit, while his crew went into action. Big Art, Lil Shooter, and Lil Snoop went toe to toe with pistols, as well as JoJo, who missed every shot. Savage felt blood in his hands as he held Britt, who was about to black out. He had no clue she was hit.

Savage yelled for help. He grabbed Big Art's pistol and took control, while Big Art carried Britt to the limo to get her to the hospital. Savage shot two of the gunmen in the chest and Lil Snoop hit the other one, who was hiding behind a mailbox, in the neck.

The last man took off his mask and jetted off. When Savage saw that it was Killer, he chased him, blasting the gun. One of the shots hit Killer in his left leg, but he still managed to get away.

"Police, give me the guns," Lil Snoop yelled, as he took all the guns and ran into the parking lot. The cops chased him, thinking he was the killer.

Lil Snoop hopped on his bike and took off with all the guns in a book bag. The motorcycle was no match for the slow cop cars.

Savage hopped in the limo and rushed Britt to the hospital. She didn't have a pulse. Minutes later, they pulled into the emergency entrance.

The nurses and doctors rushed to Britt's aid, trying to get a pulse. They shocked her four times. Her white dress was now all dark red. Savage watched them work as they rushed her into the ICU section, still trying to get a pulse.

Savage was now in the waiting room, with his goons, pacing back and forth.

"Randall, oh my god," Ms. Jackson said, coming out from the ICU area with puffy eyes. "I'm so sorry," she said, hugging him. She had been his neighbor since he was a baby.

"Britt just got here, Ms. Jackson. She will make it. They're trying now. Hold on, how did you beat me here?" he asked, confused.

"Baby, I don't know Britt. It's Lisa. She's dead, but the baby made it. He's pre-mature," Ms. Jackson said, right before everything went black and Savage passed out in the hospital.

To Be Continued...
Life of a Savage 2
Coming Soon

Submission Guideline

Submit the first three chapters of your completed manuscript to ldpsubmissions@gmail.com, subject line: Your book's title. The manuscript must be in a .doc file and sent as an attachment. Document should be in Times New Roman, double spaced and in size 12 font. Also, provide your synopsis and full contact information. If sending multiple submissions, they must each be in a separate email.

Have a story but no way to send it electronically? You can still submit to LDP/Ca$h Presents. Send in the first three chapters, written or typed, of your completed manuscript to:

LDP: Submissions Dept
Po Box 870494
Mesquite, Tx 75187

DO NOT send original manuscript. Must be a duplicate.

Provide your synopsis and a cover letter containing your full contact information.

Thanks for considering LDP and Ca$h Presents.

Coming Soon from Lock Down Publications/Ca$h Presents

BOW DOWN TO MY GANGSTA

By **Ca$h**

TORN BETWEEN TWO

By **Coffee**

THE STREETS STAINED MY SOUL **II**

By **Marcellus Allen**

BLOOD OF A BOSS **VI**

SHADOWS OF THE GAME II

By **Askari**

LOYAL TO THE GAME **IV**

By **T.J. & Jelissa**

A DOPEBOY'S PRAYER **II**

By **Eddie "Wolf" Lee**

IF LOVING YOU IS WRONG… **III**

By **Jelissa**

TRUE SAVAGE **VII**

MIDNIGHT CARTEL II

DOPE BOY MAGIC III

By **Chris Green**

BLAST FOR ME **III**

DUFFLE BAG CARTEL **IV**

A SAVAGE DOPEBOY III

By **Ghost**

A HUSTLER'S DECEIT III

KILL ZONE **II**

BAE BELONGS TO ME III

SOUL OF A MONSTER III

By **Aryanna**

THE COST OF LOYALTY **III**

By **Kweli**

CHAINED TO THE STREETS II

By **J-Blunt**

KING OF NEW YORK V

COKE KINGS IV

BORN HEARTLESS IV

By **T.J. Edwards**

GORILLAZ IN THE BAY V

De'Kari

THE STREETS ARE CALLING II

Duquie Wilson

KINGPIN KILLAZ IV

STREET KINGS III

PAID IN BLOOD III

CARTEL KILLAZ IV

Hood Rich

SINS OF A HUSTLA II

ASAD

TRIGGADALE III

Elijah R. Freeman

KINGZ OF THE GAME V

Playa Ray

SLAUGHTER GANG IV

RUTHLESS HEART III

By Willie Slaughter

THE HEART OF A SAVAGE II

By Jibril Williams

FUK SHYT II

By Blakk Diamond

THE DOPEMAN'S BODYGAURD II

By Tranay Adams

TRAP GOD II

By Troublesome

YAYO III

A SHOOTER'S AMBITION II

By S. Allen

GHOST MOB

Stilloan Robinson

KINGPIN DREAMS II

By Paper Boi Rari

CREAM

By Yolanda Moore

SON OF A DOPE FIEND II

By Renta

FOREVER GANGSTA II

By Adrian Dulan

LOYALTY AIN'T PROMISED

By Keith Williams

THE PRICE YOU PAY FOR LOVE II

By Destiny Skai

THE LIFE OF A HOOD STAR

By Rashia Wilson

TOE TAGZ II

By Ah'Million

CONFESSIONS OF A GANGSTA II

By Nicholas Lock

PAID IN KARMA II

By **Meesha**

I'M NOTHING WITHOUT HIS LOVE II

By Monet Dragun

CAUGHT UP IN THE LIFE II

By Robert Baptiste

NEW TO THE GAME II

By **Malik D. Rice**

Life of a Savage II

By **Romell Tukes**

RESTRAINING ORDER **I & II**

By **CA$H & Coffee**

LOVE KNOWS NO BOUNDARIES **I II & III**

By **Coffee**

RAISED AS A GOON I, II, III & IV

BRED BY THE SLUMS I, II, III

BLAST FOR ME I & II

ROTTEN TO THE CORE I II III

A BRONX TALE I, II, III

DUFFEL BAG CARTEL I II III

HEARTLESS GOON I II III IV

A SAVAGE DOPEBOY I II

HEARTLESS GOON I II III

DRUG LORDS I II III

By **Ghost**

LAY IT DOWN **I & II**

LAST OF A DYING BREED

BLOOD STAINS OF A SHOTTA I & II III

By **Jamaica**

LOYAL TO THE GAME

LOYAL TO THE GAME II

LOYAL TO THE GAME III

LIFE OF SIN I, II III

By **TJ & Jelissa**

BLOODY COMMAS I & II

SKI MASK CARTEL I II & III

KING OF NEW YORK I II,III IV

RISE TO POWER I II III

COKE KINGS I II III

BORN HEARTLESS I II III

By **T.J. Edwards**

IF LOVING HIM IS WRONG…I & II

LOVE ME EVEN WHEN IT HURTS I II III

By **Jelissa**

WHEN THE STREETS CLAP BACK I & II III

By **Jibril Williams**

A DISTINGUISHED THUG STOLE MY HEART I II & III

LOVE SHOULDN'T HURT I II III IV

RENEGADE BOYS I II III IV

PAID IN KARMA

By **Meesha**

A GANGSTER'S CODE I &, II III

A GANGSTER'S SYN I II III

THE SAVAGE LIFE I II III

CHAINED TO THE STREETS

By J-Blunt

PUSH IT TO THE LIMIT

By **Bre' Hayes**

BLOOD OF A BOSS **I, II, III, IV, V**

SHADOWS OF THE GAME

By **Askari**

THE STREETS BLEED MURDER **I, II & III**

THE HEART OF A GANGSTA I II& III

By **Jerry Jackson**

CUM FOR ME

CUM FOR ME 2

CUM FOR ME 3

CUM FOR ME 4

CUM FOR ME 5

An **LDP Erotica Collaboration**

BRIDE OF A HUSTLA **I II & II**

THE FETTI GIRLS **I, II& III**

CORRUPTED BY A GANGSTA I, II III, IV

BLINDED BY HIS LOVE

THE PRICE YOU PAY FOR LOVE

By **Destiny Skai**

WHEN A GOOD GIRL GOES BAD

By **Adrienne**

THE COST OF LOYALTY I II

By Kweli

A GANGSTER'S REVENGE **I II III & IV**

THE BOSS MAN'S DAUGHTERS

THE BOSS MAN'S DAUGHTERS II

THE BOSSMAN'S DAUGHTERS III

THE BOSSMAN'S DAUGHTERS IV

THE BOSS MAN'S DAUGHTERS **V**

A SAVAGE LOVE **I & II**

BAE BELONGS TO ME I II

A HUSTLER'S DECEIT I, II, III

WHAT BAD BITCHES DO I, II, III

SOUL OF A MONSTER I II

KILL ZONE

By **Aryanna**

A KINGPIN'S AMBITON

A KINGPIN'S AMBITION **II**

I MURDER FOR THE DOUGH

By **Ambitious**

TRUE SAVAGE

TRUE SAVAGE II

TRUE SAVAGE **III**

TRUE SAVAGE **IV**

TRUE SAVAGE **V**

TRUE SAVAGE **VI**

DOPE BOY MAGIC I, II

MIDNIGHT CARTEL

By **Chris Green**

A DOPEBOY'S PRAYER

By **Eddie "Wolf" Lee**

THE KING CARTEL **I, II & III**

By **Frank Gresham**

THESE NIGGAS AIN'T LOYAL **I, II & III**

By **Nikki Tee**

GANGSTA SHYT **I II &III**

By **CATO**

THE ULTIMATE BETRAYAL

By **Phoenix**

BOSS'N UP **I , II & III**

By **Royal Nicole**

I LOVE YOU TO DEATH

By Destiny J

I RIDE FOR MY HITTA

I STILL RIDE FOR MY HITTA

By **Misty Holt**

LOVE & CHASIN' PAPER

By **Qay Crockett**

TO DIE IN VAIN

SINS OF A HUSTLA

By **ASAD**

BROOKLYN HUSTLAZ

By **Boogsy Morina**

BROOKLYN ON LOCK I & II

By **Sonovia**

GANGSTA CITY

By **Teddy Duke**

A DRUG KING AND HIS DIAMOND I & II III

A DOPEMAN'S RICHES

HER MAN, MINE'S TOO I, II

CASH MONEY HO'S

By Nicole Goosby

TRAPHOUSE KING **I II & III**

KINGPIN KILLAZ I II III

STREET KINGS I II

PAID IN BLOOD **I II**

CARTEL KILLAZ I II III

By **Hood Rich**

LIPSTICK KILLAH **I, II, III**

CRIME OF PASSION I II & III

By **Mimi**

STEADY MOBBN' **I, II, III**

THE STREETS STAINED MY SOUL

By **Marcellus Allen**

WHO SHOT YA **I, II, III**

SON OF A DOPE FIEND

Renta

GORILLAZ IN THE BAY **I II III IV**

DE'KARI

TRIGGADALE I II

Elijah R. Freeman

GOD BLESS THE TRAPPERS I, II, III

THESE SCANDALOUS STREETS I, II, III

FEAR MY GANGSTA I, II, III

THESE STREETS DON'T LOVE NOBODY I, II

BURY ME A G I, II, III, IV, V

A GANGSTA'S EMPIRE I, II, III, IV

THE DOPEMAN'S BODYGAURD

Tranay Adams

THE STREETS ARE CALLING

Duquie Wilson

MARRIED TO A BOSS… I II III

By **Destiny Skai & Chris Green**

KINGZ OF THE GAME I II III IV

Playa Ray

SLAUGHTER GANG I II III

RUTHLESS HEART I II

By Willie Slaughter

THE HEART OF A SAVAGE

By Jibril Williams

FUK SHYT

By Blakk Diamond

DON'T F#CK WITH MY HEART I II

By Linnea

ADDICTED TO THE DRAMA I II III

By Jamila

YAYO I II

A SHOOTER'S AMBITION

By S. Allen

TRAP GOD

By Troublesome

FOREVER GANGSTA

By Adrian Dulan

TOE TAGZ

By Ah'Million

KINGPIN DREAMS

By Paper Boi Rari

CONFESSIONS OF A GANGSTA

By Nicholas Lock

I'M NOTHING WITHOUT HIS LOVE

By Monet Dragun

CAUGHT UP IN THE LIFE

By Robert Baptiste

NEW TO THE GAME

By **Malik D. Rice**

Life of a Savage

By **Romell Tukes**

BOOKS BY LDP'S CEO, CA$H

TRUST IN NO MAN

TRUST IN NO MAN 2

TRUST IN NO MAN 3

BONDED BY BLOOD

SHORTY GOT A THUG

THUGS CRY

THUGS CRY 2

THUGS CRY 3

TRUST NO BITCH

TRUST NO BITCH 2

TRUST NO BITCH 3

TIL MY CASKET DROPS

RESTRAINING ORDER

RESTRAINING ORDER 2

IN LOVE WITH A CONVICT

Coming Soon

BONDED BY BLOOD 2

BOW DOWN TO MY GANGSTA

www.ingramcontent.com/pod-product-compliance
Lightning Source LLC
Chambersburg PA
CBHW070518260626
47161CB00004B/1579